A stable

In *Jill's Gymkhana*, Jill Crewe became the proud owner of a pony, and learnt to ride him. Now, in the second book in the series, she is parted from Black Boy and expects to have a very dull summer holiday – until she meets Bar, Pat and Mike and they set up a hacking stable at the vicarage.

Ruby Ferguson

A stable for Jill

Illustrated by Bonar Dunlop

 KNIGHT BOOKS

the paperback division of Brockhampton Press

ISBN 0 340 04139 0

This edition first published 1968 by Knight Books, the paperback
division of Brockhampton Press Ltd Leicester
Sixth impression 1973

Printed and bound in Great Britain by
Cox & Wyman Ltd, London, Reading and Fakenham

First published by Hodder and Stoughton Ltd 1951
Illustrations copyright © 1968 Brockhampton Press Ltd

Contents

1 - The cold world for me

'Hullo!' I said to my friend Ann Derry as we met after school one afternoon. 'How's the Best Dressed Child feeling today?'

For answer she pulled the hair ribbon off my plait and threw it into the road where it was squashed flat by a passing car.

'You asked for it,' she said.

We were referring to an event which had just taken place in the village of Chatton where we live and where everybody rides and there are lots of pony shows and other horsy events such as I have described in my other book *Jill's Gymkhana*.

A woman called Mrs. Beverley had had the bright idea of offering a special prize for the best dressed child rider, the idea being to add a bit of interest to the Rectory garden party in aid of mending the church steeple which it badly needed. Actually it was a frightfully silly sort of prize, but everybody seemed to get very excited over it. I decided not to compete myself, as the clothes I wear are adequate for the kind of riding I do but far from showy, but some of the girls at school and their mothers went simply crackers. For days people were talking about what they were going to wear, or else telling you it was a grim secret, and some girls' mothers rushed them off to London to exclusive tailors who usually only make for the nobility. I should think the amount of money that was spent on those tailors would have built fourteen new steeples for the church, never mind repairing the old one.

There was a girl in our school called Susan Pyke, about whom I have told you in my other book, who said she was absolutely certain of getting the prize, which was distinctly putting-off for all the others if they had believed her, but nobody did.

My friend Ann told me rather apologetically that her mother was making her enter for this Best Dressed event, and knowing Mrs. Derry I wasn't really surprised. Thank goodness my mother is much more sensible. I said to Ann, 'Well, for heaven's sake don't let her get you up as Bonnie Prince Charlie or anything like that.'

Ann said no, she was simply having new cord breeches and boots and a covert coat and a new white shirt and string gloves and a bowler, and she wasn't even trying because she thought the whole thing was absolutely potty and just the sort of thing that Mrs.

Beverley – who turned out to be Susan Pyke's aunt – would think of.

Well, when the competitors rode into the ring on the day it was terrific and more like a fancy dress parade than just child riders.

There was one girl got up in a Charles the Second huntswoman outfit, all flowing green velvet with ostrich feathers in her hat, which fell off the second time round the ring and the pony behind trod on it; and there was another wearing scarlet jodhpurs with a sort of white Hussar tunic, and then all this extra special hunting kit from the exclusive London tailors.

Everybody was gasping, and I was thoroughly enjoying myself and having a good laugh as I leaned over the rails, when Susan Pyke rode in.

She did look marvellous, all in black and with silver epaulettes and a silver stripe down her breeches, and her boots were actually patent leather and the whole thing was crowned with a woman's hunting topper and she had gloves with enormous gauntlets like a Guardsman's. She was riding her father's black horse, Punch, which was seventeen hands and much too big for her, and unfortunately she got on his neck and couldn't get back again and then she lost her stirrups and after that she didn't look so good and the judges lost interest in her.

I will say for the judges, they had good sense. In spite of it being such a silly prize they didn't lose their heads and they weren't impressed by all the glamour that people had put on. When my friend Ann Derry rode into the ring I couldn't help feeling proud for she actually was without question the best dressed child rider that you could hope to see in the whole of England. And the judges knew it. Her pony, Seraphone, a grey, was beautifully groomed and Ann rode her with the utmost confidence. From head to foot she was perfectly and unobtrusively dressed, just right, and just as I should want to be dressed if I ever rode at Olympia or with the Quorn, which I never expect I shall do.

She so obviously deserved the prize that everybody clapped, and the judges gave it to her, and it was five pounds and a certificate. But after that I used to rag her by calling her the Best Dressed Child, which always got her goat.

It was the end of the summer term and we were having exams, which are always revolting but in this case were more revolting than usual as they had been devised by some fiend in human shape.

'What was your paper like?' yelled Ann as we whizzed down Orchard Road on our bikes.

'Sickening,' I said. 'History. What *was* the Treaty of Utrecht?'

'Search me!' shouted Ann.

Then she turned off for her home and I went on to our cottage and burst into the kitchen and threw my school case on the floor. There was just time to saddle up and have a ride before supper.

Just then Mummy came into the kitchen with a letter in her hand and a strange look on her face. I knew at once that something was up though I do not claim to be physical, or whatever they call it.

'Gosh!' I said. 'Is it good or bad?'

'I don't know whether you'd call it good or bad, Jill,' she said. 'But it's rather terrific.'

My mother is very well known as a writer of children's books, and I suppose some children must buy her books and read them – or else their aunts buy them for them for birthday presents to go in the book-case – because simply huge numbers of them are sold and keep Mummy and me and the cottage and Black Boy, my pony, going; but the fact is I can't get on with them at all, they are so whimsical, and the children in them, though considered sweet, are I think perfectly revolting.

'It's books,' I said. 'It's another publisher wants another serial.'

'Oh, no,' she said. 'It's much more than that. They want me to go to America for three months, to visit summer camps and tell stories to the children. They'll pay all my expenses and give me a lot of money as well. What am I to say, Jill?'

'Why, you'll go, of course,' I said promptly. 'It'll be marvellous for you, and I'll be all right. It'll be the summer holidays anyway, and I'll make my meals when I feel like it and ride most of the day and dust every morning. It'll be fun.'

'But you can't possibly stay here by yourself,' said Mummy.

I knew that was coming. And I knew that however much I argued, Mummy wouldn't change her mind.

'Oh,' I said coldly. 'What happens then?'

'That's just the trouble. I hate to leave you, Jill, because I know you won't like –'

'Not Cecilia's!' I said. 'Oh Mummy! How perfectly foul!'

Cecilia is my cousin and an absolute blot.

'I think I'd better not go to America,' said Mummy.

'Okay,' I said, and went to the orchard where Black Boy, my pony, was waiting for me. He came to me at once and nuzzled my shoulder, making lovely snuffling noises from sheer pleasure. I stroked his neck and pretended to chew his forelock, and he said as plainly as anything, '*Are we going to ride today?*'

I knew I was being a beast, and I knew that it wouldn't be a bit of good going on being a beast because I am not the kind of person that can be a beast and be happy at the same time.

So I went back to the house and put my head in at the door of the sitting-room where Mummy was sitting in front of her typewriter looking thoughtful, and I said, 'You've jolly well got to go to America

The cold world for me 13

whatever happens, and I'll even go to Cecilia's. It can't be worse than the dungeons under the Tower of London and people lived for years in them.'

'You are a dear,' said Mummy smiling happily at me. 'I do want to go. But, Jill, there's something awful you haven't thought of and I hardly dare to say it – you won't be able to take Black Boy to Cecilia's. You'll have to leave him at the riding school. Mrs. Darcy will be glad to have him and he'll be well looked after and exercised.'

'But – but –' I stammered.

It was terrible. No Black Boy? No riding? I choked, and dashed up to my small bedroom. This was what you got for being noble. I was being noble about Mummy going to America, and I might just as well be going to a dungeon myself. On my chest of drawers were the cups I had won with Black Boy, and his rosettes made a gay pattern pinned over the mantelpiece, and I should miss the last two shows of the season and I had been nearly certain of winning the under fourteen jumping and next year I should be too old, and if you can think of anything more utterly dismal than that you don't know anything about riding.

I did my level best to look on the Bright Side, only I honestly couldn't find one to look on. There was a book of Mummy's called 'Barbie Bright-Side' about a girl who had both her legs cut off in a motor smash and got such a name for looking on the Bright Side that practically everybody in the town used to come to her and ask her to find a Bright Side for them too, and she always did.

'Gosh!' I said aloud. '*If Barbie could find a Bright Side in this she ought to get the V.C.*'

Because funnily enough it is always easier to see a Bright Side for other people than it is for yourself.

I am sorry this book is starting in such a melancholy way, but that is how things did start, though it will get a bit better later on if you can hang out so long.

To think was to act with my mother, and to make a long story short, a week later school had broken up for the holidays, and Mummy had had a letter from Aunt Primrose, Cecilia's mother, to say 'we shall be only too glad to have dear little Jill for seven weeks or as long as you like', and I was all packed for the dreadful fray.

The worst moment – here I go all dismal again – was when Mrs. Darcy's girl groom, Angela, came to take Black Boy away because one thing I had drawn the line at doing was taking him myself. I sat on the end of my bed and didn't even look out of the window to see him go and an air of heart-rending despair filled the cottage.

However I bucked up after a bit and went down and gave Mummy the farewell present I had bought for her, which was a Horselover's Calendar with a super photograph of a horse on every page and the date underneath, and I told her to keep it and bring it back for me when she had done with it.

She said, 'You've been awfully good about all this, Jill, and I want to give you a reward. We've talked about you having another pony –'

I knew what was coming then and I was thrilled. Black Boy had done awfully well for me, but he wasn't up to the higher jumps which I hoped soon to be taking when I got into the under-sixteens; and besides when you only have one pony you sometimes get let down, for instance when Black Boy went off colour the day before the Lynbourne show and I had to scratch though I had entered for everything and Susan Pyke got three Firsts and told everybody at school that I had funked it when I saw what I was up against, which was absolute rot because I had beaten her heaps of times.

So I brightened up when Mummy said that and wondered what was coming next.

She brought her hand from behind her back and in it there was a small black leather wallet.

'I have been talking to Mrs. Darcy,' she said, 'and to Martin, and they both have a good deal of confidence in your judgment. You have been very sensible and reliable, Jill, and I feel I can trust you with money. So in this wallet I have put forty pounds –'

I gasped.

'Yes, it is a lot of money,' went on Mummy, 'and I want you to give it to Auntie or Uncle to take care of for you. But I thought that if by any chance you should hear of or see a suitable pony while I'm away you would have the means to buy it. You ought to get a decent pony for forty pounds. Anyway, it will be something to brighten up your exile, and here is another three pounds for your pocket money. Now do take care of it until you get to White Ferry.'

'Oh how wizard!' I cried and gave Mummy a huge hug.

So when the taxi came for me next day I felt a bit better about going, and was already making up a story in which I went to an auction and a magnificent chestnut show-jumper was put up and it just happened that there weren't many bidders that day and I got him for forty pounds.

2 - Home life at Cecilia's

WHEN the train got to Wayfield station there were Aunt Primrose and Cecilia standing on the platform waiting for me. In the train I had taken off my hair band and combed my hair out so that it hung round my face, and in my new grey coat I walked down the platform thinking I looked at least fifteen. However Auntie P. completely ruined the effect by shouting from about twelve yards away, 'Oh there you are, Jill dear! You weren't frightened all alone on the train, were you, dear?' And several people looked round expecting to see someone about six.

Cecilia rushed up and greeted me very gushingly, and said, 'I'm so glad you've come, Jill, and tonight we're going to press flowers for my Botany album.'

Cecilia is the sort of girl who never talks about anthing but school. Actually I couldn't think of any more squalid occupation than pressing flowers when the poor things look like dried-up corpses wilting all over the place.

'At first,' said Auntie P. with a sarky sort of smile, 'we were afraid we'd see a horse's head sticking out of the carriage along with you. But you seem quite a normal little girl after all.'

'I shall never forget,' said Cecilia, 'when I was staying with you and you were learning to ride. You did look funny.'

I didn't say anything, but I made a resolution that nobody was going to look after my forty pounds but me.

We got into the car outside the station and Aunt Primrose drove. She went round the corners very suddenly without using her indicators at all, and brakes kept squealing behind us and a lorry driver shouted something and Cecilia said, 'We never take any notice of rude men.'

When we got to the house Cecilia took me up to my room, which was awfully pretty and tidy and had a fitted wash-basin which I thought was super-luxurious, as I had never been used to anything but a bathroom which everybody wanted at the same time.

As soon as she left me I opened my case and there on the top were my riding things which I had put in at the last moment, not because I had a hope of wearing them but I thought it would do me good just to look at them sometimes. I threw my jodhpurs over the back of a chair and at once the room looked homelier. Next I got out the wallet with my money and tied it in the thick cardigan that Mummy had made me put in for if it was cold, and put it at the bottom of a drawer with all my others things on top of it. I know that in books most people take care of money by putting it up the chimney or in the mattress where it is found about a hundred years later by somebody who buys the house or the mattress, but I wanted to have this myself, not my descendants.

Then I went downstairs, and I must say we had a very good tea with sandwiches and two kinds of jam and three kinds of cake. The minute tea was cleared away, Cecilia got out a big fat heavy-looking book and a box full of depressed-looking asters and things, and said, 'Come along, I can't wait a minute. Our Botany mistress is giving a prize for the best album of pressed flowers done during the holidays and I've simply got to win it. I say, can you print fairly decently?'

'Not too badly,' I said.

'Well, I'll stick them in and you can do the lettering underneath. I say! I think this is going to be absolutely smashing!'

As I said before, I cannot think of any more dreary occupation for the holidays than pressing flowers, and all I could be thankful for was that I didn't go to the kind of school where they had the kind of mistresses who were so far gone as to suggest it.

So I spent a grim and deadly evening printing things

like 'Little yellow flower name unknown found on our tennis court' under the squashed corpses in Cecilia's album, and thinking of Mummy who was by now on her way to Liverpool, and trying hard not to think of Black Boy at Mrs. Darcy's stables and perhaps missing me and wondering if I had left him for ever.

At eight o'clock Auntie P. sent us to bed, because she is the sort of person who always treats you as if you were six until you are about 22.

I got into bed with the light on and thought I would read a bit. Somebody had kindly put three books on the table by the bed, and I picked them up hopefully on the mere chance that one of them might be about horses. Then I put them back with a groan. They were all school stories, called respectively, 'The Third Form at St. Faith's', 'The Fourth Form at St. Winifred's' and 'The New Girl at St. Ann's'.

The next morning after breakfast my Aunt said to me, 'Cecilia always tidies her room *before* breakfast, but I've done yours for you, just this once.'

I could feel myself going red, as I hadn't wakened until five to nine and had leapt out of bed and hurled some clothes on and dashed down as the last echoes of the gong were dying away, and of course I had left my room in the most frightful mess like a battle-field.

'I can't imagine why you've brought your riding

things,' went on my soulless aunt. 'You won't need them here.'

'Oh, you never know,' I muttered hopefully.

'Well, I've put them in the cupboard on the landing with some mothballs. And now what are you two girls going to do? What do you usually do in the mornings in the holidays, Jill dear?'

'Ride,' I said.

'I simply cannot see any fun in that,' said Cecilia. 'I mean, just sitting on a horse while it ambles along, I mean, it's all right for anybody that's ancient and decrepit, about forty."

'Cecilia has either a dancing lesson or a music lesson every morning in the holidays,' said my aunt, 'so do you think you can amuse yourself alone from about ten-thirty to twelve?'

'Oh rather!' I said, feeling absolutely whizzo with joy at the prospect. 'I'll go for a walk.'

'Well, don't get lost,' said my aunt.

'Oh no,' I said. 'I've got a frightfully good sense of direction. Besides, I'm used to riding for miles.'

I could hardly wait for ten-thirty for Cecilia to be gone, and directly she had left I rushed out of the house and down the road before my aunt could change her mind and take me shopping. Wayfield wasn't a bad place, and though much larger than Chatton where I lived it was surrounded by country, and country always has possibilities.

I walked to the end of my aunt's road and up another road, and then to my delight I saw a lane going off at right angles, so I ran down there and into another lane which had grassy verges and high hawthorn hedges, and I began to feel quite bucked up and whistled a bit, though I couldn't help thinking, 'Oh Black Boy, angel, if you were here now, what a marvellous canter we could have along that grass. It simply made for horses and here am I without a horse.'

Just at that moment I saw a horse. It was in a field, and was only a working mare with harness galls and a plaintive expression, but when I made enticing noises she came to me and nuzzled my shoulder across the gate, and I stroked her cheeks and her neck and talked to her for a bit, though I felt very mean at having nothing to give her, and I decided to make friends with my aunt's help and get her to dig me some carrots and stuff, because actually if you care anything about horses you should never go for a walk in the country without something for them in your pockets. And that is why you ought always to wear a sensible coat or mack with pockets and not a whimsy blue thing with frills like Cecilia wore to go to her music lesson or dancing lesson or whatever it was she had gone to.

Anyway, now I had actually talked to a horse I felt better and not so exiled among the soulless heathen, and the fact that I had rescued my coat and jodhpurs from the squalid cupboard where my aunt had put them also helped. I like my horsy clothes so much, and I am sure they can feel happy or miserable just like I do, and I thought that if I wore them, I wouldn't feel so bad about not being able to ride. Of course I don't think silk dresses and things like that have any feelings.

When I had done talking to the mare I walked on, and suddenly I saw three people sitting on a gate.

They were two boys and a girl, about fourteen and twelve and ten, and they were the most miserable looking people I ever saw in my life.

3 - Horsy people at last

I SAID 'Hullo', because when you live in the country you get into the way of saying Hullo to everybody you meet, and they all looked at me, and the two boys didn't say anything, and the girl said, 'Hullo', very dolefully.

And then she said, 'Who are you?'

'As a matter of fact,' I said, 'I'm Jill Crewe. Who are you?'

'Oh, shut up talking like Alice in Wonderland,' said one of the boys. And then he said to the girl, 'She looks quite decent, Bar. I saw her talking to the mare in Hobson's field.'

'Oh golly,' I said, 'you don't mean to say you're horsy people? That would be too marvellous.'

'Yes we are,' said the girl.

'But you look so frightfully miserable,' I said. 'What's the matter?'

'You'd be miserable –' began the elder boy, and the girl interrupted, 'Oh, shut up, Pat. She won't understand.'

'If it's anything about horses –' I said.

'It is,' said the small boy. 'Dad's going to sell our pony, because he says we can't afford her.'

'You oughtn't to have said that, Mike,' said the boy called Pat. 'It's nothing to do with strangers.'

'Gosh!' I said. 'I once had a pony I couldn't afford to keep, but I did keep him, and I've got him now and he's called Black Boy, and he's won heaps of Firsts at shows.'

'What do you mean by shows?' asked Pat suspiciously. 'Do you ride at Richmond Horse Show and terrific things like that?'

'Good gracious, no,' I said. 'Only in country events, but most of the children round about where I live are pretty good on ponies.'

'We had a pony show here for the hospital last

month,' said Bar, 'and Pat won a first and two seconds on Ballerina.'

'Nice work,' I said.

'Well, what's the use?' said Pat. 'Daddy's definitely going to sell her when he and Mother come back from Gran's next month. He says we ought never to have had her.'

I pictured their father as a harsh, cruel parent with a large black moustache and cold, pale eyes.

'Our Australian uncle gave her to us before he went back to Australia,' said Mike, 'and Dad said that cricket and football stuff for school would have been more to the point because it doesn't cost anything to keep up. And now Ballerina's out at grass, and she has to be sold before the winter. And we taught ourselves to ride too out of a book called "Hints for Young Horsemen". I suppose you went to a poshed-up riding school.'

'I did not!' I cried. 'I never went to a riding school at all, except to work there. And the man who taught me to ride had to sit in a wheel chair the whole of the time he was telling me what to do, because he was in the R.A.F. and his plane crashed. And I didn't even have a stable for Black Boy.' And then I told them all about my pony and about Mummy and me, and all the weird things I had done to make enough money to feed my pony in the winter, in fact all the things I told about in my other book, *Jill's Gymkhana*.

They looked quite impressed and not nearly so miserable.

And then I told them about having to stay here at Wayfield with my unsympathetic aunt and cousin, and they were very interested and realized how marvellous I must feel to have met some horsy people like themselves when I hadn't any hope of anything but pressing flowers and listening to Cecilia yarp on about school.

'Where do you live?' I asked.

'There,' said Mike, pointing to where a church tower showed over the tops of some trees.

'That's a church,' I said.

'Of course it is, you dope,' said Pat. 'We live at the vicarage.'

I didn't really mind him calling me a dope, because I know that when you are miserable it makes you feel both savage and rude, and I thought that if their father was the vicar he probably didn't have much money after all, and perhaps he wasn't really as bad as I had imagined.

'I say,' said Bar, 'why don't you come to our house now and see Ballerina? It's only across the field.'

'Okay,' I said, and they got off the gate and opened it for me and we all started to run. It had just come to me like a flash that perhaps I would buy Ballerina and she would be the second pony I was looking for.

When we got to the vicarage I saw that it was a

huge old-fashioned house, and it had a cobbled yard at the side with stabling for several horses, but all that was in a very bad state of repair because it probably hadn't been used for about fifty years.

In a small paddock adjoining the stable yard was Ballerina, with her head over the gate looking eagerly at us as we approached. She was a very pretty bay of fourteen hands, with lovely lines and a good head, but rather delicately made compared to the animals I was accustomed to.

'Is she a good jumper?' I asked.

'Well, I think she's got a Thing about jumping,' said Pat. 'I've seen her do a clear round at four feet, and yet another time when she wasn't in the mood she simply kicked her way through everything in the under-twelves at two foot six. Mike was riding her at the time, and was his face red!'

'More often than not, she isn't in the mood,' said Mike.

So I at once decided that Ballerina wasn't the pony for me.

'Let's saddle up,' said Bar, 'and each have a canter round the paddock.'

'I'd love it,' I said, 'but not in this awful skirt.'

'Oh, you can wear my other shorts,' said Bar. 'Come in the house and put them on while the boys get the tack out.'

Well, I thought, this is a super way of spending the

morning. If anybody had told me at breakfast that I should be up on a pony my very first morning at Wayfield I wouldn't have believed it. It just shows there are horsy people everywhere, even in the deepest desert.

In Bar's bedroom, which was frightfully plain with bare boards and just a rag rug beside the black iron bed, and a wooden chair and a shelf of books with lovely titles like 'My Friend the Horse', 'Common Diseases of Ponies and How to Cure Them', and 'Riding in Britain', we changed, and Bar put on some rather mothy jodhpurs and I put on her grey shorts, and then we went down and found the boys had saddled Ballerina and Pat was up.

Pat rode like a jockey on the pony's neck, with his knees too high, but he was very showy and it was nice to see how completely he and Ballerina were in sympathy. I could understand he would get the best out of her in a competition.

Then Mike got up and had to shorten the stirrups, and he was very fussy, but he had a good seat and a straight back and when he got going he did a lovely collected trot, and I clapped.

'Now you,' said Bar.

So I mounted Ballerina, and though I wasn't accustomed to her pace or anything I found her easy, and I was very happy on her as I cantered round the paddock.

Then Bar had a turn, and I thought she was a bit bumpy, but she was clever and did a circus trick she had practised, riding first in front of and then behind the saddle without interrupting Ballerina's pace.

When I looked at my watch, to my horror it was half-past twelve and I knew I would only just have time to get back for lunch if I ran all the way.

'Can I come again tomorrow?' I yelled, and they said, 'Yes, do!'

4 - Exile or worse

I DASHED up the steps of White Ferry which is the misleading name of Cecilia's house, just as the gong was going for lunch. I hadn't even time to wash my hands, as the dining room door was open and Auntie P. and Cecilia were already sitting at the table. So I went straight in, and my aunt gave me one horrified look and said, 'Really, Jill, I can't have you coming to the table dressed like that, whatever your mother allows. Please go and change and we'll wait for you.'

Then I realized with dismay that I was still wearing Bar's shorts, and they had a lot of horse hairs on them and some whitewash which I couldn't account for.

'Sorry!' I gasped, and flew upstairs. My skirt was in Bar's bedroom and I hadn't another, so I had to put on my blue dress, and I washed my hands and did something about the parting in my hair which had disappeared in the general mop effect.

When I got down, Auntie P. and Cecilia were sitting patiently before their cold plates of soup, looking like martyrs.

'Oh, you shouldn't have waited,' I said.

'We *never* begin until everybody is served,' said Cecilia, and I felt awful and said I didn't want any soup anyway, so they drank theirs and Cecilia changed the plates and the mutton came in.

'And what has Jill been doing all the morning?' said Aunt Primrose.

'I talked to some people I met,' I said. 'Their father's the vicar.'

'Oh, I don't think so,' said my aunt. 'Mr. Mulberry is a bachelor.'

'They are awfully nice,' I said, 'and they're called Bar and Pat and Mike, and I think their other name's Walters.'

'Oh, she means the vicar of St. Mary's at Matley,' said Cecilia. 'But absolutely nobody goes to St. Mary's. We go to St. Jude's.'

'They were jolly nice,' I said, 'and they ride too.'

Cecilia and her mother exchanged pained glances, and Cecilia said, 'A girl at the dancing class told me there are some unusual purple flowers growing by the mill-dam over the fields. I think we'll go there this afternoon and get some, Jill, for my collection.'

I had had such a good morning that I thought I could cheerfully face an afternoon with Cecilia, and after lunch we set out to walk while she gaily gabbled on about school and the mistresses and the games and how many marks she had got in all the exams.

'I thought tonight we'd just read,' said Cecilia, who had the most potty habit of planning in advance what she'd do instead of letting things happen. 'Did you bring a book? If not I'll lend you one I've just finished called "The Spirit of the School". It's frightfully good.'

'Actually,' I said – which was a word you weren't supposed to use at my school under the fifth form – 'I have got a book. It's called "Recollections of a Woman M.F.H.".'

'Oh, you are crazy about riding!' said Cecilia. 'Some time I'll introduce you to some friends of ours who know absolutely all there is to know about riding. Of course I could ride myself if I wanted to. Someone – I forget who it was – once told me I look splendid on a horse. I suppose you either do or you don't.'

'Do or don't what?' I said.

'Look well on a horse. I'd have a horse with spirit, anyway. I can never understand those people who go along like a funeral.'

'By going along like a funeral,' I said, 'I suppose you mean riding at a collected walk. If ever you see anybody doing that it means the rider has perfect control of the horse, and until you can do a collected walk you're not fit to be in charge of a horse in any public place.'

'Oh well, different people have different ideas,' said Cecilia. 'I have ridden once or twice and I found it frightfully easy.'

'Like when you were staying with us,' I could not resist saying, 'and you got up on Black Boy and bounced about all over the place and then fell off backwards.'

Cecilia went scarlet and said, 'I naturally wasn't prepared to be put on a rough, untrained pony, and then he reared and threw me. Everybody knows that no well bred pony ever rears.'

'He never reared before or since,' I said hotly. 'The way you went on he must have thought he'd got a mad gorilla on his back, or something. Poor old Black Boy.'

'You and your silly pony,' said Cecilia scornfully.

'Oh shut up,' I said. 'I'm not going to have a row. Let's go and get these potty flowers.'

So we picked flowers, and I was quite sorry for the ones I picked because they were going to be pressed by Cecilia, and all the evening I read 'Recollections of a Woman M.F.H.', and Aunt Primrose said, 'Can't Cecilia find you a really nice book?'

Next morning to my delight I had a letter from Mummy to say she was just going on the boat and had posted me some more handkerchiefs from

Liverpool because I lost such a lot; and another from
Angela who worked at Mrs. Darcy's Riding School
and was looking after Black Boy.

Angela wrote:

'DEAR JILL,

'I thought you would like to hear that Black Boy has
settled down all right and is eating like a horse (joke!). I
sent him out today with the eldest Holmes girl who as
you know rides jolly well, and she was very keen on him
and said, was he for sale? I said, "You'd better not say
that to Jill Crewe or she'll go up in flames". So she said,
"Oh is this Crewe's pony that did so well at Chatton
Show? Well, don't you let anybody ride him but me till
Jill comes back." So you see he'll be well taken care of.

'I have just finished the grooming and feeds, and it
reminded me of what fun it was that time you worked here.
I am actually sitting on an upturned bucket waiting for
Mrs. Darcy to come back so I can go off duty. She has
gone in the shooting brake to see a pony at Forder.

'Are you getting any riding? I can't imagine you not
doing, it would be worse than death. Yesterday I took
Cocktail over to North Spinney, we went by the fields and
she simply sailed over everything, it was grand. I thought
of you.

'So no more now,
'Love from ANGELA.'

As I read this nice letter and pictured the fields at
home and the sun sparkling on the hedges and horses

flying over timber with inches to spare, I gave a gulp, and unfortunately a piece of toast I was eating popped right across the table and went ping against the silver marmalade jar. I wanted to giggle, but Auntie P.'s eyes went enormous and Cecilia just looked pained and began to cut her toast into tiny little bits and put them into her mouth with frightfully exaggerated daintiness. I thought how differently people take things like that, and how Mummy would have giggled too, though we hadn't a silver marmalade jar for anything to go ping against and it would have hit our ordinary grocer's glass one and given out a feeble pong.

This made me feel exactly like the Irish exile in the song, and I thought what fun it was at home at the cottage, getting up early to muck out the stable and feed my pony, and then dashing in to find the kettle boiling all over the place and taking Mummy up a cup of tea, and then eating my porridge with all the enthusiasm of a starving sailor, and Mummy coming from the hens and saying, 'Gosh, isn't it marvellous, Martha's laid again!'

Compared with Cecilia's luxurious home some people might think mine squalid, but I thought it was mighty fine, as Big Bill Campbell says. You jolly well don't appreciate things till Fate ruthlessly snatches them away from you, so if any of you who read this book think it is pretty grim at your home doing all the usual things every day, wait till you go and stay with some relations who do everything properly, and you'll see what I mean.

I made a silent vow that as long as I lived neither I nor any of my descendants would have anything on the table so soppy as a silver marmalade jar.

When breakfast was over, having nothing else to do I looked out of the window until half-past ten when the hour of my release approached and Cecilia came out of the drawing-room with her music case, all ready to go to her lesson.

5 - Ideas about Ballerina

'I've been thinking about you people all night,' I said to Bar as she greeted me at the vicarage gate.

'I'm jolly glad you've come,' she said. 'I thought you might be a bit fed up with us and not bother. And Agatha said, where did that skirt come from and where were my shorts.'

'Who's Agatha?' I said.

'She's our housekeeper that looks after us when Father and Mother are away. At least she calls it looking after, but we call it the iron hand in the iron glove.'

'You mean the velvet glove,' I said.

'Velvet my foot!' said Bar. 'Is that newspaper parcel my shorts?'

I handed them over, and said, 'You should have seen my aunt's face when I dashed in to lunch with them on, all horse hairs and whitewash. I don't know where the whitewash came from.'

'Oh, all my clothes have whitewash on,' said Bar. 'Your skirt's in the kitchen.'

'Good,' I said. 'I'll change out of this awful frock, and actually I've brought my jodhpurs and a sweater, they're in the parcel with your shorts.'

Then Pat and Mike came running out, and we all went and leaned over the paddock gate like horsy people do and chewed straws and looked at Ballerina.

'As I said,' I began, 'I've been thinking about you people a frightful lot in the silent watches of the night and all that sort of thing. You do want to keep Ballerina, don't you?'

'Want to?' said Mike. 'What do you think!'

'Well,' I said, 'there's only one way. You've got to show your father that she isn't going to cost him anything to keep. She's got to be self-supporting. You've got to turn her from a frozen liability into a profit-producing asset.'

'Gosh!' said Pat, staring at me in admiration; and Bar and Mike said together, 'How?'

'Well, what can you do with a horse to make money?' I said.

'We did once think of a circus,' said Bar, 'and getting people to pay to come in, but we couldn't get enough turns. I can do three different tricks on Ballerina, and Pat and Mike thought they might practise jumping on and off bareback, only we didn't have any clown's clothes and I asked Mummy if I could cut up the spare room curtains – I mean, nobody ever uses the spare room, and they are sort of yellow and black check – but she said no. So that idea died on us, and we haven't thought of anything else.'

'You might use her to give a few lessons,' I suggested, 'if there are any kids about here who want to learn to ride.'

'Oh help!' said Pat. 'We can't ride well enough ourselves to teach anybody else. We'd get put in prison.'

'Actually there are kids,' said Bar, 'but I don't think we'd be very hot as teachers. I wouldn't even know how to tell a kid to mount a pony.'

I looked at her doubtfully, as I had read somewhere that teachers are born and not made and I suppose that applies to riding as well as maths and things.

'Well,' I said, 'if you don't know how to tell anybody how to mount a pony you jolly well ought to get a book and learn. Stand on his left side, by the shoulder, with your back to his head. Place the reins in your left hand and put it on the withers in front of the saddle. Next take hold of the stirrup with your right hand and place your left foot in up to the instep, and then take hold of the waist of the saddle with your right hand. Then spring from the right foot –'

'You can write it out for me some day,' said Bar, and I blushed and said, 'I wasn't showing off.'

'Oh cut it out, you two!' said Mike. 'The circus is off and the riding lessons are off, so what do we do now?'

'Let's go and have our elevenses,' said Bar. 'It may give us an inspiration.'

So we went in the house, and the elevenses proved to be very good indeed, consisting of coffee and hot toast with jam on, because the Walters' Agatha, though lacking in what you might call endearing qualities, Believed In Food.

'There's one thing about us,' said Bar, 'we're always willing to learn. If there's anything wrong with my riding I hope one of you will always tell me. I have a dread of getting ham-handed, because someone once told me that people who are naturally light-handed are so sure of themselves that they grow hammier and hammier as they get older. You can go on for ever learning something new about riding, can't you? Even when you're the Pride of the Quorn, and all that.'

'My cousin Cecilia,' I said, 'says she knows some people who know everything there is to know about riding. They must be blots, mustn't they?'

'Of the first water,' agreed Bar. 'I suppose your cousin wouldn't have any ideas about making a horse self-supporting?'

I gave her a withering look, and Pat said, 'We are a dumb crowd. There *must* be something you can do with a perfectly good pony. In the old days, if a man had a horse that seemed to be all he needed.'

'Are you suggesting we should be highwaymen?' said Mike.

'I wouldn't mind having a stab at that,' said Pat, 'only we'd have to do a bit of explaining to the Pater if we came staggering in every night dripping with gold watches and diamond rings.'

We stuck our elbows on the table and thought.

Looking idly out of the window, I said, 'Gosh, you've got some marvellous premises here. When I was a kid about two years ago I used to say the dream of my life was to keep a stable. You could keep a smashing stable here. There's room for six horses.'

'Well, what do you do with your stable when you've got it?' said Pat. 'Sit and look at the horses? Or just tie ribbons in their foaming manes?'

'You're so frightfully funny,' I said, 'I wonder you don't die laughing at yourself! Near us at home there's a woman called Mrs. Darcy who has a stable. Actually she's looking after my pony while I'm here. She runs a riding school, and she hires hacks, and she's got a most lovely foal that was born in the stable and she's going to sell him when he's older. I'd be content just to have a hacking stable, because I love grooming horses and cleaning stables and I once did it professionally at Mrs. Darcy's when I needed some money for my own pony.'

They all looked at me with awe and respect, and Bar said, 'Well, that sounds all right, but we can't do much with only one horse, even if we have got stables. And you should see the inside of them! Talk about the dirt of ages! Ballerina's stall is the only decent one.'

'I know what I'd like,' I said dreamily. 'I'd like to see a notice on your gate saying, "Hacks for Hire".'

'Well, stick one up,' said Mike cheerfully. 'If anyone comes to hire one we can trot Ballerina out and say, "unfortunately this is the only hack I have in the stable at the moment, sir", which would be quite true.'

'Too Blooming True,' said Bar.

'I don't want to hurry you,' said Pat, 'but it's nearly twelve o'clock.'

'Oh, how sickening!' I groaned. 'I'll have to go.'

'Come on!' said Bar. 'Let's have a canter first. You can have first go, Jill. And could you show me how you do that figure of eight?'

So we dashed into the paddock and did figures of eight on Ballerina, more or less correctly, and then I really had to go.

'Do see if you can come this afternoon,' said Bar. 'I'm sure we shall think of something if we have more time.'

I didn't think there was a hope of this, but as you know, grown-ups are quite unpredictable, and my aunt said, 'Well, I want you to stay in this afternoon, Jill, as some people are coming to tea who know your mother; but as you are going to be here for several weeks it won't be a bad idea if you can find some means of amusing yourself. I've been making inquiries, and the Walters children seem to be All Right.'

'Oh, thanks most awfully,' I gasped, and flew upstairs to write to my friend at home, Ann Derry.

'Dear Ann,' I wrote, 'You will be glad to hear that things are not so grim as I thought they were going to be. I have been lucky enough to make friends with some horsy people and once more we are up against the old problem of Ways and Means, like I was with Black Boy. Can you think of any ways of making One Horse self-supporting? If so, just send me the details.

'How is Seraphine? I hope that swelling on her hock went down, in time for the Bank Holiday show. I am dying to know what happened, but if Susan Pyke won the jumping you needn't tell me or I shall die of rage. Did your kid sisters enter for the under-tens Showing class on their Shetlands? I bet they looked sweet.

'You might pop up to Mrs. Darcy's some time when you've nothing to do and take an apple for Black Boy. I'd give everything I've got for just one good ride.

'Love from JILL.'

In the evening my uncle came home from London where he had been on business and said that for a treat he would take us to the pictures, as Auntie P. said there was a picture that was suitable for young

girls. What she meant was, suitable for kids, as it was
a very weepy picture about a kid of ten who lived in
dire poverty in a slum in the Big City. This kid was a
marvellous singer, and the funny thing was that
whenever she burst into song either in the street or in
her dirty kitchen, a fifty-piece orchestra would pop
up from nowhere and accompany her. This kid had
a dog she adored, a St. Bernard weighing about half
a ton, and I couldn't help wondering how her parents
who were so poor could afford to feed it. Well, one
day this dog got run over and killed in the street, and
it was rather unfortunate that this was the day when
the kid was having an audition at the Opera House,
with Cartoni, the great impresario. She was so upset
about the dog that she made an awful mess of the
audition, and Cartoni was furious, thinking he had
been brought all that way to hear a kid that couldn't
sing for toffee. So out she went into the snow, but
somebody told Cartoni about the dog and he was
filled with remorse and went after the kid. He arrived
at her meagre home to find her scrubbing the floor,
at ten o'clock at night, and crying great big blobby
tears that stuck on her face, and singing bits out of
La Bohème so beautifully that he just rushed at her
and cried, 'A new Star is born'. The next thing, she
was singing La Bohème at the Opera House and a vast
audience was clapping, and when it was over she put
on a long white ermine coat and the impresario hauled

up a new St. Bernard dog (which I think was the same one as I particularly noticed its markings) and she put her arms round its neck and sang 'Stille Nacht'. And that was the end.

I found I was very unpopular when we got outside, as I had giggled in all the bits where I saw the funny side of it, as Mummy and I always did when we went to the pictures together, and my aunt and Cecilia had both cried.

6 - Three more horses

THE next morning I went haring off to the Vicarage, feeling particularly thrilled because I had the whole day in front of me and my lunch that I had begged from my aunt's maid, in a parcel. I had on my jodhpurs and a fawn sweater with a turtle neck that Mummy had knitted, and I didn't even care when Cecilia said, 'I shouldn't think it would do your marvellous riding any good to ride on any poor old broken-down horse that the Walters might have. But you should know.'

It was a cold day for August and the sky was grey, but I was happy and I whistled as I ran, and thought of my unfortunate mother battling with the raging main and hoped she was finding some consolation in looking at the magnificent pictures [in the Horse-lover's Calendar.

When I came in sight of the Vicarage I knew something had happened because Mike was standing up on the wall looking out for me, and as soon as he saw me he jumped down and ran off to tell the others, and when I got to the gate they were all there.

'Bags I tell her!' shouted Mike. 'I say, Jill, we've got three more horses!'

'What!' I gasped.

'Three more horses!' shouted Mike. 'We'll be able to start the stable now.'

'It's this way,' said Bar. 'We have an uncle we call Uncle Toots, who's a vet and lives about two miles from here. He's been ill and has gone away for two months and left a locum at his house, but he's also left three horses out at grass in his field, and before he went he said sort of jokingly to us, "You can give those horses a bit of exercise if you feel like it", but of course we didn't bother about it at the time and it had slipped our memory. But the point is, we can *have* those horses if we want them. Nobody wants them while Uncle Toots is away.'

'How absolutely gorgeous!' I said. 'Why, we can start a stable straight away.'

'The snag is,' put in Pat, 'that there are horses and horses.'

'What do you mean?' I said, with visions of gorgons and other monsters floating before my eyes.

'Pat means,' said Bar, 'that as riding horses these of Uncle Toots' aren't so hot, so don't get any idea of shining hunters or even decent ponies like Ballerina. In the first place, there's Bungie who's twenty-seven. In the dim, dark ages he was Uncle Toots' riding horse; now he's pensioned off. He sags in the middle just like a hammock, and half the time he's fast asleep. But on his best days, which are few and far between, he's just rideable. Then there's Mipsy, the cob that pulls the trap, because Uncle Toots is old-fashioned and won't use a car. He always glares at me and shows his teeth, and actually nobody can do much with him but Uncle Toots. And then there's Dot, the Shetland, that Uncle Toots' daughter grew out of. And that's the lot.'

She sounded more than doubtful, but to me horses were horses, the most wonderful creatures in the world and full of exciting possibilities, so I said at once, 'Can we go and see them? *Now?*'

'Yes, let's,' said Pat who was always practical. 'Let's go on the bikes. I'll ride Mike's with Mike on the crossbar, and Bar can ride mine and Jill can have Bar's.'

So we whizzed off to this place of their uncle's, and as we got there we saw a car standing at the gate and the young locum was just coming out in a white lab-coat, with a spaniel under his arm.

'Hullo!' said Bar. 'We've come to have a look at the horses out at grass, if that's okay by you. Uncle Toots said we could exercise them if we liked.'

'It's okay by me,' said the young vet. 'Help yourselves.'

'And if we thought of taking them away to our place?' said Bar.

'Nobody's using them but you,' said the young vet, placing the spaniel very carefully on the back seat of the car, as it had a splint on its off-hind leg.

So we went round the side of the house and across the yard, where there was a long row of out-buildings from which issued interesting noises like the yowling of bored cats and the yapping of dogs and the bleating of sheep. I thought it was all fascinating and would have liked to have a look at the patients; in fact I decided at that moment it would be rather fun to be a vet as a sort of side-line to the stable I meant to run some day. But there wasn't time to stop, so we went straight to the gate which led into the field, and there were the three horses.

The old horse was quite near by, standing under an oak tree with his eyes shut and slightly swishing his tail in a vain effort to discourage the flies. He was a nice chestnut with black mane and tail, but his head was very bony and heavy and he certainly sagged in the middle, very hammockishly.

The cob, also a chestnut but with a curious effect as though a bottle of ink had been sprinkled over his withers, stood a little way from us and looked at us with a suspicious eye, then lifted his front lip and whinneyed at us.

The Shetland, who was grazing on the far side of the field, didn't even bother to look up. She was a nice little animal with good lines, but too fat.

'Well, there they are,' said Pat. 'What do you think of them?'

'Of course they're not exactly bloodstock,' I said, 'but I do think they've got possibilities. For instance, the Shetland is an asset in any stable. Kids love riding on a Shetland, and the mothers think they're so sweet and innocent, though they sometimes have quite awful dispositions – the Shetlands, I mean, not the mothers. Then the old horse might be useful if we get a very nervous client who wants something quiet and steady. By the way, I never asked, but are the cob and the old horse broken to the saddle?'

'Oh yes,' said Bar. 'The old horse used to be Uncle's riding horse about a hundred years ago, and he bought the cob from a farmer who used to ride him.'

'What about tack?' said Mike.

'Well, Dot has her own, and Bungie's old saddle must be somewhere around, and I know there's loads of stuff lying about in the harness room. Come on, let's see.'

So we went to the harness room, which was full of all sorts of things like old kitchen chairs and medicine bottles and a pram and a pile of fire-logs, and we discovered the Shetland's saddle and a snaffle-bridle and a double bridle much the worse for wear, and also Bungie's tack which was filthy, and an odd saddle that would do for the cob, and two more bridles, and some stirrups that looked as if they had been at the Battle of Waterloo, and some mothy-looking rugs, and a box of dirty dandy-brushes and other cleaning things, and a tube for blowing pills down horses' throats, and a lot of other things all mixed up with the dust of ages.

'Crumbs!' said Pat. 'How are we going to get all this junk to our place?'

'It's going to be even crumbier getting it clean,' said Bar. 'But actually that carrier – what's-his-name Evans – would fetch it for us cheaply. Let's drag all we want out into the yard!'

So we did, and by this time we were filthy and jolly hot. Then we went into the harness room again and poked about looking for halters, and we found three very dirty and knotted ones in a box labelled 'Glass With Care'.

'Come on, let's get the horses,' said Mike. 'They'll take some catching after being out at grass for two weeks.'

'Listen,' I said. 'This has got to be properly done in a professional way as befits people who are going to keep a well-run stable. Before we take the horses we've got to tackle those stables at your house. They're not fit to put a gorgon into.'

'Well let's take the horses now and put them in our paddock with Ballerina,' said Pat.

'Look at them!' I said. 'They've got to be clipped before we can begin to groom them, and probably re-shod. Is there a place near where that can be done?'

'Oh yes,' said Bar. 'There's the farrier's nearly opposite. We could tell him to carry on with the horses while we're getting the stables ready. But the point is, who's got any money?'

'I can raise about fifty pence,' said Pat, and Mike said he had thirty and Bar said it was a pity but she'd have to take something out of the Post Office.

I said, 'We'll wait till the farrier's bill comes in and then divide it between us. We'll have to keep some books and put down all our expenses and takings.'

'Takings!' said Pat. 'Ha. Ha. Ha.'

So we went across to the farrier's, and he said he would collect the three horses and clip them and replace any worn shoes, and give us a ring at the Vicarage when they were ready, and then it was half-past twelve and we thought we'd done a jolly good morning's work, so we biked back to lunch.

After lunch – at which I added my sandwiches to the general mêlée – we thought we would go out and have a look at the grim and ghastly sight which lurked in the stables.

This was even worse than the direst dreams of a fevered imagination could depict. (I got that out of a library book, and copied it in my notebook to use sometime. Whenever I use really highbrow phrases like that, they are out of my notebook and the fruit of some distinguished author's gigantic brain, not mine.)

In the first place, the Vicarage stables didn't even smell of stables, which is – I think – a beautiful and inspiring smell. They smelt of dirt and spiders and cats and old sacks. That is, all except the small one where Ballerina had her stall, and even that wasn't up to my standards. And when we got inside you could understand why they smelt of dirt and spiders and cats and old sacks, because that is what they were mostly full of. I shouldn't think they had had any horses in them or been cleaned since about the year Queen Victoria came to the throne.

'Gosh!' said Mike. 'It's past hope.'

'Not it,' said Bar. 'It's just a terrific job, isn't it, Jill?'

'Okay,' I said. 'Now we've got to get cracking on this. This afternoon we'll pull all the old sacks and things out and make a bonfire of them. Then we'll pool some money and buy cleaning things and white-wash. And then we'll jolly well all four go at it till the stables are fit to put our horses in. And after that we'll have all the tack fetched from your uncle's and clean that. It's about a week's solid work, I should say.'

'Let's go in the house and make a list of the cleaning stuff,' said Bar.

So we went in and made a terrific list, beginning

with scrubbing brushes and ending with saddle soap and metal polish, and as ready money was needed for these we pooled what we had and the boys offered to go to the hardware shop and do the buying.

I promised to be round early to start the good work, and with that I took my leave and departed from my nice, horsy world to the dreary pink-cushioned one in which I was doomed for a time to wilt.

I washed and changed for dinner, and in the evening mended my string gloves and hoped I should soon be needing them.

7 - Walters and Crewe Ltd

Next morning we got right down to work on those awful stables. We were wearing the weirdest assortment of garments, in fact any rags that we could unearth, and we had ransacked a box in the attic of the vicarage which was really intended for bombed-out civilians, but that seemed a bit out of date anyway and the things could all go back when we'd done with them, if nobody minded a few spiders, sploshes of whitewash, and large damp patches of a peculiar-smelling chemical stuff called Stablo which is meant for cleaning out stables and proved to be jolly good.

First we lighted a bonfire and burned all the rubbish. It was a bit unfortunate that Agatha had just washed some pillow-cases and hung them out to dry, and the result was heated words on both sides, but as we obviously couldn't move the bonfire she kindly agreed to move the pillowcases, and they weren't really very smoky and would probably look quite clean when dry.

Then we got up on ladders and washed the walls down – this was an awful job as all the water which had been on the walls descended on us and we couldn't wash for spluttering – and when this was done we swilled all the floors with hot water and Stablo and brushed them with yard brushes.

Then we left everything to dry, and that was a whole day's work.

The next day we whitewashed, and that was another whole day's work; in fact I had to go before it was finished and the others nobly carried on all the evening while I languished in the hated bonds of social life, handing round cups of coffee to some friends of Cecilia's who had come to talk about starting a School Madrigal Club. When they had sung a few madrigals, a girl called Phyllis Barnes said to me, 'Which do you like best?' and without thinking I answered, 'White-wash,' and Cecilia said, 'Don't take any notice of her, Phyllis, she isn't quite all there.'

But on the whole Cecilia was glad to get rid of me in the daytime, so that she could go out to coffee with her friends and practise the piano for some school-prize that she wanted to win, and write letters to one of the mistresses that she had a crush on.

Meanwhile the stables were finished and a credit to us, and we got a plumber in to make the taps work and a man to clean out the drain which proved to have a family of mice in it, and we set to work like mad, cleaning tack. We banged clouds of dust out of the saddles, and then we brushed them and soaped them and rubbed them up, and we did the same for the leathers and the girths and bridles, and then we polished all the bits and the stirrups – and it took hours to get the dirt off, never mind putting a shine on them – and then we washed all the dandy brushes and stable rubbers and other things and arranged them neatly on the shelves, and we arranged the tack in the cleaned-out harness room after we had shunted the Vicar's old books out of it, and we had now been at it for five days and were ready for the horses.

It was a great moment when we walked over to Uncle Toots' to fetch them. The farrier had made them look quite decent and put them back into the field, so we paid his bill, and by then everybody but me was insolvent. In fact I had such terrific faith in the stable idea that I thought I might as well go the whole hog, and I had ordered a lot of fodder from the local corn merchant, hoping that we should have made some money before the bill came in.

Bar, Pat, and I each took a halter and Mike acted as rounder-up. We got the Shetland easily because she was too fat to move away from us, but the cob led us an awful chase as he was very nappy after a few weeks off work; and Bungie the old horse was also a problem, because though we got the halter on him he just didn't get the idea of moving and it was like trying to shift the Pennine Chain. Though as a general rule I never hit a horse and think nothing of riders who use crops in the show ring, on this occasion there was nothing else for it, so I cut a hazel switch and gave Bungie just one flick on the flank, and he jumped as though I had put a squib under him and gave me the look of a Victim to its Murderer. However he ambled off, and then Mike running beside him did his circus trick and leapt on to Bungie's back. There he sat, grinning and waving, and looking so like a monkey in a sailor's hammock that Bar and I could only giggle.

So we got the horses home, and though Pat and Mike were all for saddling up and trying them, Bar and I said no, they must have a chance to get used to their new home first, so we opened the gate of the paddock and shoved them in. Ballerina looked most haughty and resentful, just as you probably would if someone unceremoniously opened the door of your house and shoved in three rather weird-looking strangers, but after a bit her curiosity became too much for her and she sidled up to Mipsy and they began to graze together. Dot didn't bother at all, but found a nice spot and planted herself in it as though she belonged, and Bungie just stood inside the gate and went to sleep.

By now it was lunch-time, but we were too excited to bother much with food and golloped it down, and unfortunately Mike choked and was sick and Agatha made him lie down on the kitchen sofa.

The next thing was to try the horses. We collected

them, and got them saddled, which wasn't as easy as it sounds as they weren't a bit keen on the idea after their lazy life at Uncle Toots', and then I being the lightest went on Dot while Bar mounted Mipsy and Pat took old Bungie.

I found that Dot wasn't too bad at all. She had at one time been properly schooled and the vet's daughter who rode her must have known something about the principles of horsemanship, and Dot even obeyed my diagonal aids quite nicely; but Bar wasn't having such a good time on Mipsy. Mipsy was just silly, bucking and shying, showing his teeth and pretending to be a poor little nervous horse, which he certainly wasn't, but after a bit he realized that Bar knew what she was doing and he settled down. He had never been properly schooled, but he knew enough to be a decent hack for anybody who could ride. As for Bungie, he turned out better than we had expected. There were only three things about Bungie, Start, Walk, and Stop, but when Pat got him started he went on walking until made to stop, and he wasn't stubborn or awkward about it, so we thought he would do quite all right for any client who wanted a really quiet horse.

Then Mike came out feeling all right again, and Bar mounted Ballerina, Mike took Dot, I took Mipsy, Pat stayed on Bungie who seemed to like him, and with Ballerina leading we went round and round the paddock as though it were a riding school, making our horses do more or less what Bar did on Ballerina.

Thus the afternoon slipped away, and finally we took the horses to their nice clean stalls, rubbed them down, and fed them.

'That's all for today,' I said. 'Now what about tomorrow?'

'Grand opening,' said Pat, and we all dithered with excitement. 'Look here, we boys will muck out, and then you and Bar can take over.'

'That's jolly sporting of you,' I said. 'And I'll come early in time for the feeding, and then there's all the grooming to do. I vote we open in the afternoon.'

So I dashed off, and by the time I got home I was nearly too tired to crawl, but fortunately for me

Cecilia wanted to spend the whole evening practising her prize piece so I was able to go to bed early.

I arranged with Doris, my aunt's help to call me at seven and I was quite prepared in my enthusiasm to cut out breakfast, but Doris proved to be a really super person and called me with two cold sausages and a pile of bread and butter which I ate while I was putting on my new yellow shirt and jodhs and tying my fawn tie.

I then scribbled a note to my aunt which read,

'Dear Aunt Primrose, please excuse me from breakfast as I have to go out on business. I will be sure to be back about five. Love from Jill.'

I dashed downstairs and put this on the dining-room table, then I collected the sandwiches which the worthy Doris had been making while I dressed and I simply flew, before anybody could stop me.

When I got to the stable I beheld a scene of terrific activity. All the mucking out had been done, and Pat and Bar had already started the feeding. So we finished that, and then we were ready to groom our four horses.

First we washed all their sixteen feet and then we got to work with the dandy brushes and by the time we had finished that we were all scarlet in the face with exertion and excitement and working at top speed, quite apart from the fact that Mipsy and Dot didn't want to be groomed and you know what that means! Ballerina was an angel and a great help, holding up her feet for Bar to wash them while Pat and I struggled to make Mipsy bend his joints.

'Could you by any chance lay your hand on a few soap flakes for their tails?' I said. 'I always have to get mine at home when Mummy isn't looking, as she thinks that soap flakes are destined for higher things than washing horses' tails.'

'I can do better than that,' said Bar. 'If we can get Agatha out of the kitchen I'll pinch her liquid shampoo. It's wizard for tails.'

'I'll go into my bedroom,' said Mike, 'and yell out to Agatha to come and find my other shirt, and then you can nip into the kitchen.'

This worked like a charm, and once Agatha was out of the kitchen Bar got in and found the liquid shampoo in the corner cupboard. It was called 'Gleemit' and there was a picture on the bottle of a most beautiful girl with millions of shining curls, and it said underneath, 'You too can have hair like this if you use "Gleemit" regularly.'

I doubted this, and certainly Agatha's hair wasn't in the least like the beautiful girl's, but the shampoo turned out to be marvellous for horses' tails and we thought when we had time we would write and tell the makers who would probably be glad to know and could use it in their advertisements.

Finally Mike, who was good at making wisps – which isn't a bit easy and actually quite a gift – made some wisps, and we finished the horses off, and we left them standing with their tails drying and they really looked very nice indeed. The whole place looked frightfully clean and efficient, and I wouldn't have cared if Mrs. Darcy herself had inspected it, in fact I wished she could.

Then we took off our rags and put on our riding things, and Bar and Pat and Mike had awfully nice breeches and boots that they had spent the money on that their Australian uncle had given them for tips when he left, though their mother wanted them to spend it on dreary tennis and football kit that you have to have for school in any case. Bar and Pat had white shirts and Mike had a blue one, and we tied our ties with great care and brushed our hair.

Finally I produced my surprise. A few days before I had bought some cartridge paper and some Indian ink at an art shop, and in my room in the silent watches of the night I had made a big placard which read:

```
WALTERS AND CREWE LTD

HACKS FOR HIRE
```

The others said they thought this was simply smashing, so we got a hammer and some tacks and went out and nailed it up on the oak tree by the gate of the stable yard.

Mike didn't know what LTD meant, so I explained that it meant this was a proper business to make assets, not just a game.

As I had a bit of cartridge paper left over I had done another little thing, with a drawing of a horse and rider flying over a five-barred gate and underneath the pleasant words:

> Hands down and head up,
> Heels down and heart up,
> Knees close to your horse's sides,
> Elbows close to your own.

This we tacked over the stable door where our clients would be able to see it.

Then we went in and had lunch, and Agatha said, 'I don't know what your Mum and Dad would say, but I suppose it isn't my business,' and Pat said, 'We couldn't agree more.'

8 - People want to ride

AND then when everything was ready and we were actually waiting for the clients, you will hardly believe it but we all had an acute attack of the needle and started quarrelling like mad.

Bar began it by telling Mike for goodness' sake to keep out of the way when any clients arrived, as they might not think much of an establishment that had people in it who were only ten; and I stuck up for Mike and said that he had done his share of the work and Bar was just being beastly on purpose; and then Pat stuck up for Bar and told me that considering it was *their* stable and *their* horses, wasn't I throwing my weight about far too much? And I said, whose was the idea of the hacking stable anyway, and who had made all the suggestions? And if it wasn't for me they'd still have been feebly sitting on a gate moaning about having to part with Ballerina, but if that was how they felt I knew what to do, and I began to stride towards the gate, but Pat yelled after me, 'Come back! I apologize!' and Bar said, 'Oh, do shut up, everybody. You know it's only because we all feel like just before you go into the ring at a show.'

Then Pat remembered that he had left the tap running, and Mike said there was a pitch-fork just where anybody would fall over it when they went into the harness room, so they both went off, and Bar said, was her hair all right and would she look older with a hat on? And just at that moment a very tall, oldish, military-looking man in tweeds came into the yard.

We both gasped, and the man came up to me and said, 'Anybody in charge here? Jolly glad to see I can hire a horse here occasionally. Left all mine in India.'

'We're in charge,' said Bar quite coolly. 'Anything we can do for you?'

He looked a bit taken back, and said, 'Well, I want something up to my weight. Well-mannered, and not a slug. Do you charge by the hour?'

Will you believe it, in all the excitement of getting the stable and the horses ready that was the one thing we had never discussed, what we should charge! So I had to think awfully fast and make these world-shaking decisions alone.

I looked at Bar but she just gaped helplessly back at me, so I thought a minute and then said, 'We charge twenty-five pence an hour, or sixty-five for a whole morning or afternoon, or a pound a day if you want to go for a riding picnic.'

'Well, let's start with one hour,' said our client, looking a bit grim. 'What have you got?'

'Excuse me while I speak to my partner,' I said, and Bar and I walked a few yards away.

'We daren't show anybody like him anything but Ballerina,' she said.

'Why not Mipsy?' I said. 'He's stronger than Ballerina.'

'Yes, but it's one of Mipsy's bad days. He nipped Pat while he was mucking out.'

'Well, let's show them both,' I said, 'and trust to luck.'

So Bar and I led out Ballerina and Mipsy, and Ballerina looked all smug and lady-like, but Mipsy made faces and pecked, and I was ashamed of him.

'I'm afraid this is all we have in that would suit you,' I said to the client. 'You see, we didn't actually expect –'

'This establishment actually only caters for children,' said Bar in a very dignified way.

'Good heavens!' said our client, looking at the animals, and added, crossly. 'Of course those won't do. The mare is a lady's pony and I couldn't possibly see myself on a cob. Your notice says Hacks for Hire. If what you mean is children's ponies you ought to say so.'

And away he went without a backward glance.

'Well, that's that!' said Bar. 'What a beast! Do you think all our clients are going to be as beastly as that?'

Then Pat and Mike who had been in the harness room and had heard every word came out, and Pat said, 'We ought to get some money from somewhere and buy one decent horse, a hunter or something. This is just *playing* at keeping a stable,' and I was furious and said, 'All right, you get out and we'll play at keeping a stable by ourselves,' and Bar said, 'Oh, shut up!'

'While we're on the subject,' I said, 'I do think we ought to change the horses' names. I mean, I can't think of any more utterly revolting names for horses than Mipsy and Bungie and Dot. I mean, it's so mean-minded to give horses names like that. They ought to be called Starlight and Cameron and Gay Girl, or something like that.'

'Well, you can call these horses Starlight and Cameron and Gay Girl till you're blue in the face,' said Pat, 'but they'll never answer to anything but Bungie and Mipsy and Dot. They're too old.'

'Well, I shall call them Starlight and Cameron and Gay Girl to the clients,' I said.

Bar giggled.

'Can't you just see one of our clients saying, "Come up, Cameron" to Mipsy?'

'Oh look!' shrieked Mike. 'There's somebody coming! A mother and a little boy.'

Sure enough, a very fashionable-looking mother all in grey with a red hat with birds on, was coming into the yard holding the hand of a kid of about six in a beige coat and gloves.

We all brightened up, especially when the mother who said her name was Mrs. Charles asked if we had a nice, gentle little Shetland that would do for her little boy, who was a lovely little rider and missed his own pony very much while they were staying at Wayfield.

So of course we led out Dot, and Mrs. Charles said, 'Get up, dear,' and the little boy struggled into the saddle in a rather sack-like manner, and Mrs. Charles said, 'Doesn't he look adorable? I'd like to engage the pony for the whole week that we're here.'

Bar said, 'You'll water her and rest her well, won't you? And please bring her back each day before five.'

And Mrs. Charles said, 'Oh, of course. Cecil goes to bed in the afternoons in any case, so he'll only actually be riding for a bit in the morning and after he's rested, but he'll like to feel the pony's there, just like his own at home.'

So I said, 'Well, we charge a pound a day, but we might make a bit of a reduction for a week,' and Mrs. Charles smiled and said, 'That's quite all right.' And off they went.

'Nice work!' yelled Pat and Mike together.

'Isn't that smashing?' I said, multiplying a pound by five, six, and seven, according to how many days Mrs. Charles called a week. 'It'll be five pounds at least!'

'Five pounds!' said Bar in an awed voice. 'Why, the stable's practically supporting itself already.'

However, nobody else turned up, and about half an hour later Pat said, 'We really ought to have taken Mrs. Charles' address. Suppose she makes off with Dot and never brings her back!'

At this grim thought we went cold all over, and were frightfully uneasy for the rest of the afternoon, but to our relief at five minutes to five Mrs. Charles and Cecil arrived back with Dot, and Mrs. Charles said, 'Well, we've just had the afternoon and we'll be back for Dot tomorrow morning early, so shall we wait till the end of the week and I'll give you a cheque?'

We were so thrilled that when she was gone we went quite mad and did a sort of circus all round the yard, and then we brought in the horses and fed them and I went home.

To make a long story short, Mrs. Charles and Cecil had Dot out for five days running, and on the fifth evening she said, 'Well, tomorrow will be our last day as we are leaving for home,' and I said, 'We'll get the account ready for you when you come tomorrow.'

But she didn't come tomorrow; in fact she didn't come any more, and we never saw or heard of Mrs. Charles and Cecil again. What was more, when we tried to ring up the hotel where she said she was staying the exchange told us there was no such hotel.

This was a revelation to us, as we didn't know there were such beastly people in the world, and Mrs. Charles probably thought she had been very clever in getting a free pony for her little boy for five days and an afternoon and then disappearing, just because we didn't look very old or experienced. But actually, though we were awfully sick when we thought of the five pounds we ought to have had, we were very sorry for poor little Cecil too for having such a beastly mother.

But meanwhile we hadn't been doing too badly. There were two very nice sisters called Diana and Brenda Prince who had been out three times on Ballerina and Mipsy, and a rather shy boy called Bill had been out on Bungie because he was just a beginner and his father who went with him wanted something awfully quiet for him, and an older girl of about eighteen who was dancing at the local theatre had taken Ballerina out four separate hours and rode beautifully, and a school friend of Pat's had taken Mipsy out once, and if only we had had Dot free we could have used her several times for small children. So at the end of the week we did have some money, and we were solvent as it says in books.

9 - Stable trouble

'WHAT on earth do you do all the time at that place?' said Cecilia one day.

'Oh, just mess about with horses,' I said with a frightfully cool shrug of my shoulders.

But I could see that she was simply eaten up with curiosity, so I wasn't surprised when she said, 'I want to come and see what you do,' and as I was actually staying with her and had to obey the binding laws of hospitality I couldn't say, 'No, you jolly well won't!' so I just said, 'Okay,' and hoped she'd forget.

When I got down to the stable I found everybody in a state of fuss over Mipsy. It had been wet the day before and he had been out with a boy friend of Pat's and had got thoroughly messed up, so Pat had spent ages that morning grooming him and had then told Mike to lead him up and down the yard to air off. But Mike had suddenly thought of something he wanted to do, and had popped Mipsy in the paddock by himself, whereupon Mipsy made for that muddy spot under the trees and laid himself down and *rolled*.

Gosh, you should have seen him!

Pat was engaged in flattening Mike, and Bar was saying, 'What shall we do? He's got to be ready for an hour with the Parker boy, and look at him!'

'I'll do him,' I said. 'I'm fresh. You get the others ready.'

So I set to work with the water-brush, meanwhile telling Mipsy just what I thought of him, and I did his eyes and nose and ears which were all muddy, and I finished him with a wisp and a rubber, thanking goodness that he was docked, though as a rule I don't approve of docking as I think it is cruel to deprive a horse of his natural fly-whisk, and I gave him a final slap just as the Parker boy came into the yard.

'Phew!' I said, for I was boiling hot and jolly well aching too. But I couldn't help thinking how beautiful the stable yard looked in the morning sunshine, with the doors open to show clean stalls and the shining horses waiting for their riders.

Just then Mike came up to me and said, 'There's a girl outside asking for you. I think it's that Cecilia.'

It was Cecilia all right.

'Good gracious!' she said, gazing round with a look of astonishment on her face and walking backwards into Ballerina, who was standing ready for work and obviously hated being walked into.

'Oh, hullo, Cecilia,' I said without enthusiasm.

'Good gracious!' she said. 'You are dirty.'

'So would you be,' I said, 'if you had just been grooming a muddy pony.'

'Oh, do you do that?' she said. 'I do think Mummy would be furious. I can't imagine anybody liking to do such dirty things.'

'Well, some people do,' I said.

'What is this horse waiting for?' she went on, and Bar who had just come out of the harness room said, 'It isn't a horse, it's a mare.'

'Well, it's all the same,' said Cecilia. 'Can I have a ride?'

'What time is Ballerina booked for?' I asked Bar, who replied that Diana Prince would be coming round in a quarter of an hour.

'You can try her in the paddock for about ten minutes,' I said to Cecilia, 'and for goodness' sake don't make her hot.'

So Cecilia, who had terrific ideas about her riding, scrambled up on Ballerina – I cannot call it mounting – and suddenly slapping her heels upon the poor animal's unsuspecting sides, dashed off into the paddock at a pace that nearly unseated her.

'Does she usually ride like that?' asked Bar.

'Oh, always,' I said. 'She calls it proper riding. She hates people who walk along as if they were at a funeral. She thinks, what's the use of a horse unless he's galloping?'

So we both laughed, and then were busy getting a girl called Hilda Southwood – a beginner – off on Bungie and a small child called Noel Something-or-other on to Dot, while his Nannie stood by saying, 'Upsy-daisy, Nannie's little man,' which we thought was too revolting for words, though you have to be very tactful when you are running a stable and not laugh at the clients.

Then we started cleaning tack, of which there was always some waiting to be done, until Diana Prince looking awfully nice in fawn jodhs and a hacking coat of brown tweed came in at the gate, all ready for Ballerina.

'Hey! Where's that cousin of yours?' said Bar.

I had forgotten Cecilia, and I had just said, 'I'll go and find her,' when a horrible sight appeared at the gate of the paddock and my veins turned to ice, as it says in one of Grimm's fairy tales or elsewhere.

I honestly couldn't tell which was Cecilia and which was Ballerina, they were both so plastered with mud. Cecilia's legs and skirt and blouse and face and hair were just one solid lump of mud, and as for Ballerina! The only place on Ballerina that hadn't got mud on it was the part round her mouth and she was actually smirking, I suppose because she had successfully played up Cecilia.

'This b-b-b-beastly h-h-horse!' sobbed Cecilia, who was weeping real tears which trickled stickily off her muddy nose. 'He – she – it took me to where there was some mud and threw me into it and then rolled on me! It's a hateful horse. It ought to be shot!'

'Don't be silly,' said Bar in a fury. 'Ballerina couldn't possibly have rolled on you or your ribs would be broken. If she threw you, why didn't you get up and stop her from rolling? Look at her! Who's going to jolly well clean her, I should like to know?'

'You are the limit, Cecilia!' I said. 'Right-ho, Bar, I'll do Ballerina. Cecilia's *my* cousin, and I might have known.'

'It looks as though my ride's off today,' said Diana Prince. 'I can't come this afternoon instead, so I'd better leave it till tomorrow.'

'There!' said Bar, as Diana walked away. 'That's fifty pence gone.'

'Can Cecilia go in your bath?' I said. 'I know she's a blight, but she can't go home like that.'

'Okay,' said Bar, 'I'll take her,' and off she walked followed by the blubbing Cecilia, dripping mud as she walked.

You can guess how I felt at being confronted with yet another mud-plastered pony. However I carried on manfully, feeling that one's relations are one's own responsibility and *noblesse oblige* and all that. After about three-quarters of an hour Cecilia came out, clean and wearing a skirt and jumper of Bar's, and with a long scratch on her nose, and said, 'Fancy taking money for giving people rides on ponies! I wonder you don't go on the sands.'

As a consequence of this, I was not surprised when later that afternoon Auntie P. said to me, 'I was rather surprised to hear that you and those children at St. Mary's Vicarage are actually giving children rides and taking money for it. I'm sure your mother wouldn't like that. I mean, it simply isn't the sort of thing that I should let Cecilia do.'

'As a matter of fact, Aunt Primrose,' I said, 'we are not giving children rides. We are running a proper hacking stable, and Mummy says there is nothing to be ashamed of in running a proper business concern.'

'Well, I think you're a very odd girl, Jill,' said my aunt, 'and I don't know if I ought not to forbid you to go to that place any more.'

I was so horrified at this prospect that I flew upstairs and sat on my bed for ages, thinking. Then I scrabbled about in my drawer and found a bit of paper and composed a cable to Mummy, and after altering it about ten times to make it less words, it finally read, 'HAVE GOT HONEST WORK RUNNING HACKING STABLE KNOW YOU WOULD APPROVE ALL FOR A GOOD CAUSE PLEASE PLEASE TELL AUNT I MAY. JILL.'

I then rushed downstairs and ran all the way to the Post Office where I handed in my message, and then ran all the way back, only to find that the tea gong had gone in my absence and I wasn't even changed, which made me rather unpopular.

I will say for Cecilia that she hadn't said anything about getting thrown by Ballerina into the mud, as I had feared she would make a terrific story about it – savage, unschooled ponies and all the rest of it – but I think she was really a bit ashamed of herself. I don't know what it was about Cecilia, but there really are some people who bring out the worst in horses and she was one. I mean, Ballerina was a well-mannered pony and had never before in her career even *wanted* to do such a thing as rolling in mud till Cecilia got her; and it was just the same with my pony at home who actually reared for the first and last time in his life when Cecilia was up.

All the next day and the next I was in such a frantic state of suspense that my teeth simply knocked together, and when the cable from Mummy actually arrived my numbed fingers would hardly open it, as it says in novels.

But I might have known Mummy would be all right!

The cable just said, 'HAVE FAITH IN YOU DO RIGHT THING CARRY ON WITH HACKING STABLE BUT CONSIDER AUNTS FEELINGS IF POSSIBLE. MUMMY.'

I was so thrilled that, left to myself, I should have rushed all over the house making hunting cries, but

I thought I had better consider my aunt's feelings, so I showed her the cable and said, 'I honestly don't want to be a nuisance, and please tell me if I do anything wrong, Aunt Primrose,' and she said, 'Well, if your Mother says so I suppose it's all right,' and I felt so awfully pleased and forgiving that on my way home from the stable that afternoon I went into town and bought some wool to start knitting a pair of Fair Isle gloves for Cecilia in my room in the silent watches of the night.

The stable was now doing very well, and we had paid ourselves back what we originally put into it and could pay the corn-merchant's bill and regular expenses like shoeing. We had started a new idea, for very small children who could have half an hour on Dot for 12½p, being led round the paddock by Mike, and some children came every day for this with their Mummies or Nannies.

Of course the stable was by now not a game but jolly hard work. Every day we had four horses to feed and groom, to say nothing of mucking out and keeping the stables clean and cleaning all the tack. We started work at eight every morning, after the boys had mucked out, and we were busy until about five. Wet days were our despair, because really keen riders went out in all weathers and brought the horses back wet and splashed, and if you know of anything worse than being confronted by one or two really messed-up ponies when you want your tea, I'd like to know what it is!

But of course that is all part of keeping a stable, and to be absolutely frank and honest I was beginning to cool off a bit from the idea of having a stable of my own for ever and ever.

10 - How not to buy horses

I HOPE you have not forgotten the pony money which my mother had given me on the occasion of our dismal and sad parting. What I really wanted to buy with this money was a show jumper, but I hadn't had time to think about looking for one and anyway there didn't seem much chance of finding one in the neighbourhood of Wayfield. Besides I had another idea in my mind. As Pat had once said, the stables were theirs and all the four horses were theirs, and though I am sure he didn't intend to be mean and probably forgot the words as soon as he had said them, I sometimes remembered them in the silent watches of the night. which as you may have noticed elsewhere in this book I often refer to. After all, I called myself a partner in the stable but I hadn't actually given anything to it compared with the Walters'. What I was thinking was that some of our clients had said their older brother or sister would have liked to come for a ride if we had

had a horse big enough for grown-ups, and Pat had said it was a pity we hadn't anything in the hunter class.

Well, about two o'clock one morning I woke up suddenly and decided I would buy a horse of about 15–16 hands, and use him in the stable, and then sell him again. I thought it would be a rather noble thing to do and would please Bar and Pat frightfully.

I then went to sleep again, and when I woke up properly in the daylight this still seemed a good plan, which was unusual, as things you plan in the middle of the night generally seem perfectly idiotic in the morning.

When I told Bar she thought it was a splendid idea, and Pat said, 'There's a sale of horses at Farbury next Thursday. I saw it advertised. Let's send for a catalogue.'

So the catalogue came and there were actually about sixty lots, though I think it is most squalid to call such wonderful creatures as horses 'lots' even when they are in a dreary sale-room.

We pored over the catalogue. I don't know what pored means, but people always do it in books. I think it means leaning right over the table and breathing on the paper, like we did.

'Gosh!' said Bar. 'Listen to this. "Grey hunter, Albatross, 17 hands, 3 years, from Earl of Sattingham's stable, by Hercules out of Ocean Bird –".'

'That'll be about three hundred pounds,' I said, 'unless there's something wrong with him.'

'There'll be something wrong with him or they wouldn't be selling him at Farbury,' said Pat. 'How about this one? "Bay mare, Strawberry, 15 hands, 5 years, has hunted –",'

'I don't like "has hunted",' said Bar. 'It sounds jolly sinister to me.'

'That sounds a good pony,' I said, pointing to "Grey pony, show jumper, 14.2, four years, spirited, one owner", and wondering whether I had been a bit too rash in promising to buy a hack for the stable instead of a pony for myself.

'But we don't want a pony,' said Pat. 'Oh, look here! "Lot 36. Chestnut mare, Begorra, 16 hands, 15 years, ridden by lady, very sound, useful hack." I wonder how much she'll fetch?'

We talked a lot more, and then decided that Bar and I would catch the 9 o'clock bus for Farbury on Thursday morning which would get us there about 9.45 and give us time to look over the horses before the sale started at 11.

I was there by ten past eight, and we began to get ourselves ready. We thought this was very important, as we wanted to look thoroughly hard, experienced horsy people who couldn't be taken in. It was a very hot day, and I had on my jodhpurs and boots, and a clean white shirt and my fawn tie with foxes' heads.

Unfortunately I couldn't do much with my hair as it looked worse out of plaits than in them, but I put on some lip-stick that I had bought for the occasion at Woolworth's and then I asked Bar how I looked.

'Well, quite honestly,' she said, 'you only look about thirteen, which you are. You'd better try my best coat and skirt.'

So I got into the grey coat and skirt which was a bit too big for me and rather long, and made me look much older, and I put on my string gloves, and Bar found a pair of sun-glasses with tortoiseshell rims and pushed the dark glass part out, and I put them on and when I saw myself in the mirror I did look very impressive.

Bar had on her breeches and boots, in spite of the heat, and a tweed coat with leather patches on the elbows, and her bowler, and she had frizzed out her hair a bit at the sides and used my lipstick, and she looked marvellous and about sixteen.

The boys thought we looked jolly good and that one look at us would make the auctioneer realize what he was up against, and then Pat said, 'Have you got the money, Jill?'

'Of course,' I said. 'It's folded into a handkerchief and pinned inside my jodhpurs with about seven safety-pins.'

'But you haven't got your jodhpurs on!' said Mike.

'Oh help!' I yelled, and tore back into the house

and up to Bar's room and found my jodhpurs and unfastened the safety-pins, and my fingers were all thumbs. Then I had to do them all up again to fasten the money inside the lining of my coat, and that made us late for the bus and we had to run all the way and just caught it as it was moving, so for about five minutes we could only lie back on the seat panting with our mouths wide open; and it was a bit of a blow for us because when the conductor came and I gasped, 'Two returns to Farbury, please,' he said, 'Do you want halves?'

'What do you mean?' said Bar haughtily.

'Under fourteen half fare,' said the conductor, and before we could stop him he had clipped them. It was more humiliating for Bar than for me because she was actually fifteen the next month.

When we got to the sale-rooms and saw all the horses waiting to be sold to any hard-hearted and unscrupulous purchasers that might come along, I wished I was a millionaire so that I could buy them all and put them into lovely paddocks, but when I told Bar this she said, why should I think that other purchasers were any more hard-hearted and unscrupulous than we were? So it was a bit more comforting to look at it like that.

'It's no good wasting time looking at things like Albatrosses and children's ponies,' said Bar. 'Let's look for ones that would be useful to us.'

So we walked along the rows of horses and ponies which were all tied to rings in the dirty walls, and we stopped when we saw anything we liked. Actually, we were afraid that anything we wanted was going to be too dear for us, because I had decided that I wouldn't spend more than about thirty pounds. We passed the farm horses and the tradesmen's cobs, and then Bar said, 'Here's Number 36 that Pat read out. She looks rather decent, doesn't she?'

She did look decent, and though she was fifteen years old she had nice, clean lines and a lovely clear eye, and when I went to examine her legs and feet she nuzzled me gently and I could tell that somebody had once been very fond of her. I began to make up a story about her mistress having died, and a soulless lawyer thrusting poor Begorra into the cold world to be sold until I nearly started weeping.

'Seems all right,' said Bar in a most reassuring horsy kind of way. 'Do you think there's something wrong with *all* horses at *all* sales?'

'Oh, there couldn't be,' I said, 'or really intelligent people wouldn't buy them would they? – and some of the people here look frightfully intelligent.'

'When does the auction start?' Bar asked a man who was standing near, and he said, 'It's started, Miss. He's sold fifteen lots already.'

We had been so busy looking at the horses that we hadn't noticed a small crowd gathered round the auctioneer at the far end of the room, which wasn't really a room at all but a sort of long tram shed.

'Oh, come on, Jill,' shouted Bar. 'We may have missed something.'

However we weren't interested in what was being sold for a long time, though we learnt a lot from watching other people bid.

Albatross went for a hundred pounds, which seemed to worry the auctioneer quite a lot as he kept telling the buyers that this hunter was worth at least four hundred, which I don't think could have been true. He had a mean-looking head and no hocks to speak of.

I was interested in the grey pony, the show jumper, because though I had purposely not examined him for fear Bar would think I was trying to get out of my bargain, I couldn't help thinking he might have done for me. It was almost a relief to me when he fetched sixty pounds, more than I could have given in any case.

'Here's ours!' whispered Bar excitedly, as a groom led Begorra out and began to show her paces up and down before the crowd. 'I say! We never looked at her teeth. She may be fifty, not fifteen. Are we going to bid for her?'

'Yes,' I said. 'I like her. Sssh! He's started.'

'Now here's a nice animal,' said the auctioneer. 'Best bargain of the show, I call this. Fifteen years old but been well looked after. Absolutely sound, nice action – look at that, ladies and gentlemen. I've seen animals in the hunter class no better than that fetch seventy pounds.'

'Oh help!' said Bar.

'It's all right. He doesn't mean it,' said a rather nice, oldish man who was standing next to us. He looked as if he knew a lot about horses, and I suddenly whispered, 'Oh, do please tell me. Do you think that's a good mare?'

'What do you want her for?' he whispered back.

'Hacking stable,' I said, excitedly.

'She'll do nicely,' he said.

'Now somebody start me for this fine mare,' said the auctioneer. 'Best hack I've seen in years for her age and description. Anybody start me at thirty pounds?'

'Ooooh!' Bar groaned.

'Twenty pounds?' said the auctioneer, and I shouted out, 'Yes!' at the top of my voice.

Everybody turned round to have a look, and a rather harsh voice at the front said twenty-one. Then somebody else said twenty-two, and I got thoroughly worked up and said twenty-three and about two minutes later I was saying twenty-eight, and there was only me and the harsh voice left in the bidding. He said twenty-nine and I said thirty, and thought, oh dear, this is the fatal end. Then there fell a grim hush, and just as I thought it was all over the man at the front said thirty-one in a faint, hesitating sort of voice.

'Go on!' said Bar. 'You can tell he's shot.'

So I said, 'Thirty-two,' awfully firmly, and this time the pause lasted several seconds longer and then the auctioneer crashed down his hammer and looked at me and said, 'Name please.'

I was too overcome to utter a sound, but Bar called out very coolly, 'Walters and Crewe, St Mary's Stables, Wayfield.'

The auctioneer looked very impressed with this splendid-sounding address.

'Congratulations!' said the nice man next to me. 'You've got a bargain.'

'I call that super,' said Bar. 'Let's go now.'

So we went to find the place where you paid, and I felt an awful fool unpinning all those safety pins to get my money out when other people just brought out wallets bulging with notes or wrote cheques.

Anyway, Begorra was mine, and it does give you a wonderful feeling to have bought a horse all by yourself.

'How do we get her home?' said Bar to one of the grooms.

'If you've got the tack you could ride her, if it isn't too far,' he said, but we said we couldn't do that, and in the end it was arranged for Begorra to be delivered by van next day, and we paid in advance

for this, because I like to know how much I was spending all at once.

I threw my arms round her neck, and we both made a fuss of her, and you could see that she liked us, and she said as plainly as anything while I stroked her neck, 'Thank you for buying me. I know I'm going to be awfully useful to you,' and I said to Bar, 'Wouldn't it be marvellous if her dead mistress could see what a good home she's going to?' and Bar said scornfully, 'What on earth are you talking about?'

We felt wonderful when we came out of the dark and smelly sale room, and we decided to go and have some lunch at a café before going home.

'I hope that hasn't ruined you completely,' said Bar as we sat over the sausages and chips. 'I think it's jolly decent of you to have done it – we all do – and it will be a great asset to the stable, and after all you can sell Begorra again and probably make more than you gave. I think you'd better let the stable stand the one pound for transport.'

'Okay,' I said. 'With what I've already spent and the thirty-two pounds, that leaves me – six pounds.'

So after lunch we went round the shops at Farbury which weren't very good and bought some hair grips and things, and then we went to the bus.

11 - And as for Pedro -

I DON'T know what you feel about it, but I always think that on days when anything terrific happens, something else terrific happens almost immediately after. I mean, you go on the same old round of school and eating meals and having a ride before you start your homework for days and days and even weeks and weeks, and all of a sudden something happens to you almost as though you were in a book and before you get your breath something else – if you see what I mean. I mean, I think it was a pretty terrific thing for me to go and buy a horse for thirty-two pounds, but if anybody had told me that before the day was over – but I'd better get on with it.

When we got off the bus Bar said she'd better go to the cake shop and get some buns for tea, so I waited outside for her. And right opposite where I was standing at the kerb-side was the poorest, dirtiest pony I ever saw in my life. I couldn't help staring at him because he was so wretched, and it made a little cold feeling start in my middle and work right up to my neck. You couldn't see what colour he was, he was so dirty; and yet in spite of it all, and in spite of his miserable, downcast head, he had nice lines and good legs and I think it was partly that which made me look at him and think what an awful pity it was he was so neglected.

He was harnessed with filthy, string-mended harness to a little cart with a few sticks of firewood on it, and on the side of the cart was painted in very dirty paint, J. Biggs. Timber Merchant.

Just then J. Biggs himself came out of the pub, and he was just as dirty as the cart and the pony, but they couldn't help it and he could.

The first thing he did was to say a horrible word, and then he picked up the reins which were trailing in the gutter – which was his fault – and lashed the pony across the face with them. Then he gave it a bang on the flank with his fist, and it staggered and slipped and he gave it another bang.

Well, I don't know what you would have done, but you can do all sorts of things when you lose your temper that you wouldn't dare to do in cold blood, and I rushed at the man and said, 'Don't do that, you beast.'

He looked very surprised, and I said, 'I've a jolly good mind to fetch a policeman.'

I think he would have said a few things to me then, but a man who was passing stopped and said, 'Good

for you, little girl,' and a lady also stopped and said,
'Poor little pony! It looks half-starved. He ought to
be reported. Take his name and address.'

Just then Bar came out of the cake shop and said,
'What on earth's going on?'

'Oh Bar!' I gasped. 'Did you ever see such a poor
miserable pony? And he's sweet, too. And this
horrible man –'

Seeing that everybody was against him, the horrible man thought it was time to change his tune, so he said in a wheedling voice, 'I'm sorry, miss, I lost my temper a bit. You see, I'm a poor man and I've had a lot of trouble. I've got a sick wife and seven hungry kids at home, I have.'

'Well, you've no business to hit that pony –' I began, and Bar interrupted, 'You don't deserve to have a pony. People like you make my blood boil.'

'Well, it's like this, Miss,' said the man, 'I had to take this 'ere pony as part of a debt and he's been a bad bargain. No use to me in my business, he isn't. He's a dead loss, as you might say. Don't understand kindness, he don't. I have to nearly kill him to make him go at all, I do.' And he turned round as if he was going to hit the pony again, just to show us.

'Stop!' said Bar; and at the same time I heard myself saying, 'You shan't take him away and beat him. I'll buy him from you. How much do you want for him?'

Bar and the man both stared at me, and the man found his tongue first and said, 'Well, I'd want a good lot for him, you know. I'm a poor man, I am. Five quid I'd want for him.'

'All right,' I said. 'Here's five pou – I mean, quid.' And I took my six pounds out of my pocket and peeled off one and held out the rest to him. This is the sort of thing you do when you're in a blazing temper.

The man looked absolutely thunderstruck, I suppose thinking he had suddenly come across a millionaire child, and said, 'Did I say only five quid? I meant seven –'

'Oh no, you didn't,' said Bar, and some people who were standing by said, 'You said five quid! Take the money and give the little girl the pony!'

'Well I'm blowed!' said the man, only he didn't say blowed.

'Get him unharnessed,' I said, 'and we'll make a halter out of that bit of dirty rope on the cart and take him with us.'

'But what am I going to do with the cart?' said the man, and some people in the crowd which had by now assembled said, 'It wouldn't hurt you to push it home yourself.'

Actually I think he was awfully glad to get the five pounds, and just at that moment a policeman came along and began to say, 'Pass along, please,' and believe me, in about two minutes everybody had melted away, including the man and his cart, and there stood Bar and I with the dirty pony between us and the end of his dirty rope in my hand.

'We're both absolutely mad,' said Bar. 'Here, Butterfingers, let me make that into something like a halter.'

'I know it was mad,' I said as we walked towards home, rather slowly to accommodate the pony which seemed bewildered, poor little thing, 'but I simply had to do it. Something made me.'

'I'd probably have done the same, if I had five pounds,' said Bar. 'Gosh! Let's get home quick before we buy any more horses!'

It was only about a mile, and when we came in sight of St. Mary's Vicarage we saw the boys in the garden on the look-out for us. As soon as they caught sight of us they came running, and if you had seen their faces when they beheld Bar and me, one on each side of that wretched pony! It dawned on us they must be thinking that was what we had bought at the sale!

'No, no!' shouted Bar, and I yelled, 'We didn't buy it, this isn't it; I mean, we did, but it isn't, I mean it's coming tomorrow, not this one, the proper one!'

We got into the yard at last, and the pony seemed thankful to stand still, shivering a little and looking miserable, his head hung down. The boys gathered round, and somehow between us Bar and I managed to tell the whole tale of the day's adventures.

'I think you did quite right, Jill,' said Mike, walking round and round the pony. 'And I think he's a nice pony – if he was clean and you could tell what colour he was. If I had a million pounds I'd do nothing but buy poor ponies like this one, and I think five pounds was jolly cheap. I bet the man stole him and was glad to get anything for him before he was caught.'

'He isn't small, either,' said Pat, 'about 14 hands

if he wasn't so sort of wilted.' And he put his arm round the pony's neck and began to stroke his nose. The pony flinched as though he expected to be hit, but he stood still and seemed to be slightly enjoying it. He even turned his head and had a look at Pat out of what would have been a lovely eye if it hadn't been so bloodshot and messed up with flies. Pat found a lump of sugar in his pocket and held it out for the pony, but the poor thing didn't seem to know what to do with it, which we thought was awfully touching.

'What are you going to do with him now?' said Bar.

'Well, is it all right if I put him in the box stall at the end?' I said. 'I mean, it's your stable.'

'Why, of course!' said Bar. 'He's going to live here, isn't he, boys – as long as Jill wants him to?'

'You bet!' said Pat and Mike.

'Thanks most frightfully,' I said, because after all it *was* their stable and I had wished this poor pony on them. 'I'm going to put him in the stall with heaps of clean straw, and give him a bran mash and leave him to rest until tomorrow. He'll feel better by then.'

'Goody!' said Mike. 'I'll go and fetch the straw.'

So we made the stall very comfortable, and we put the pony in, and he looked more bewildered than ever but just a bit pleased, and I fed him. He only hesitated a minute, and then he began to eat. Eat! I got frightened, and tried to slow him down, but I hadn't the heart to stop him really though I was a bit afraid he would swell up and burst during the night.

'Well, that's that,' said Bar as we fastened the door and came back into the yard. 'And we've hardly talked about Begorra at all!'

'And how's business been today?' I asked.

'Quite good,' said Pat. 'Dot did children's rides for two hours this morning and went out for an hour this afternoon with the Burton kid and its Nannie. And Bungie is out with that Irish girl who likes him because he's so quiet, and I've been schooling Mipsy all afternoon and he's booked for the day tomorrow. And Ballerina is still out with Brenda Prince. And there'll be an awful lot of competition for Begorra, because absolutely everybody's big brothers and sisters want to ride. Everything's mighty fine.'

Of course when I got to bed that night I couldn't sleep a wink for thinking of what I had done and all the money I had spent on buying horses that weren't a bit what I wanted or what my forty pounds was intended for. I mean, fancy having forty pounds given to you by your loving mother to be spent on a show jumper and then going and spending thirty-seven of them on a fifteen year old hack and a dirty neglected pony with grazed knees and harness galls, which I regret to say my latest pony had. I sat up in bed in the silent watches of the night and I'm sure my hair was standing on end. And yet I'd have done it all again! And I wasn't worrying over only having one pound left, as the stable was doing so well and we were just about to have a share out.

I got up at seven and ate a hurried breakfast at the kitchen table, which my aunt now allowed me to do, and simply rushed round to the stable. The pony hadn't bust in the night, in fact he looked heaps better already and was holding his head up! I called Bar and Pat and they agreed that he looked heaps better, and then Mike turned up and the first thing he said was, 'I say! He looks heaps better, doesn't he?'

'First of all,' I said, 'I'm going to get the vet round to see him because I want to be sure he isn't dying of some frantic disease, and then if he isn't, we'll groom him, Bar.'

So we rang up the vet – who was Uncle Toots' locum – and he happened to be coming past our way to see a cow at one of the farms, so he called in about half an hour and saw the pony and said there wasn't a thing actually the matter with him except neglect and starvation and he thought he had the makings of a nice pony and we might be surprised some day, which was quite cheering.

So Bar and I got to work. We laid on with dandy brushes and water brushes but they didn't seem to make the slightest impression on the dirt which was simply clotted on like an overcoat. So I'll tell you what we did, though it isn't usually done in stables. We waited until Agatha went out of the kitchen and upstairs, and we pinched the soap flakes out of the scullery. We got some hot water from the scullery tap and we read the instructions carefully, and we used the whole packet of soap flakes, and the pony looked exactly like a film star in one of those foam baths. And the dirt came off in *chunks*. And underneath he was a lovely dark bay. And then we worked with the dandy brush, and we washed his feet and his nose and eyes and mane and tail, and we polished his hoofs and rubbed him up with a rubber and finished him off with a wisp, and then we just stood with our tongues hanging out, panting like dogs.

When Pat and Mike came along to look they didn't recognize him, which wasn't surprising, he looked so nice, though we couldn't disguise his thinness and the harness galls.

'And now I'm going to feed him up like anything,' I said. 'He knows me, don't you, darling?' And as I said it, to my amazement he turned his head and looked at me and then made a lovely little whiffling noise and nuzzled my shoulder. I loved him from that very minute.

'Look at that!' said Bar. 'I believe this pony's got a history. We'll never know, but I think at some time he's been cared for. And he's a *good* pony. Look how he stands – and he lifted his feet for me to wash them

as if he'd once been used to it. What are you going to
do with him now, Jill?'

'Well, I should think he's pretty exhausted after all
that washing,' I said. 'Besides, he's weak. The vet
said rest him, so he can go back in the stall and tomorrow we'll put him in the paddock while the other
ponies are out. And' – I added – 'I've just thought of
it, I'm going to call him Pedro after Pedro the Fisher-
man which I think is a jolly good song!'

Just then Pat began to run to the gate as a horse
van drew up. Begorra had arrived!

12 - Begorra is a success

WE all turned out to form a welcoming party for
Begorra, and Bar and I simply swelled with pride,
she looked so nice as she came down the ramp of the
van with her head up and just dancing a little on her
toes, and her coat was shining too as somebody had
taken the trouble to give her a rub up.

'Oh, I say!' cried Pat. 'What a smasher!'

'Doesn't she look enormous?' said Mike, and of
course she did compared with all the other horses, for
even Bungie in her prime was only 15 hands. 'I should
think a king would like to ride her.'

We took Begorra straight to the paddock which
was only occupied by Bungie as the other ponies were
being got ready to go out, and we introduced her to
Bungie and then left her to get used to things while
we got on with our job of saddling Mipsy, Ballerina,
and Dot, a procedure which seemed frightfully tame
after all the excitement.

However when our clients arrived we had their ponies ready, and I was just helping a very fat Nannie to heave an absolutely square child up on Dot when Mike came up to me and hissed, 'I say! Trouble ahoy!'

'What do you mean?'

'It's that man again,' said Mike, and looking up I saw the oldish, military-looking man who had been our first – and disappointed – client. He was just coming into the yard, and he had by the hand a small kid in a velvet crash cap and too-big jodhpurs which small kids often have to wear because their mothers can't get their size or else want them to have something to grow to.

He came straight up to me, and said very politely, 'Am I addressing Miss Walters or Miss Crewe?'

'I'm – I'm Crewe,' I said, a bit taken aback.

'We met on a previous occasion,' he said, 'and I must ask your pardon for having made a bad impression which I'm sure I did. But I've been hearing a lot about your stable, and I understand it is a well-run place. It looks clean and orderly –' he went on, looking round, '– and if there's one thing I admire more than another it is people who do something with horses and do it successfully.'

'Oh. Thank you,' I stuttered.

'You boys and girls have done a splendid job,' he went on, while I wondered if I was dreaming or had

got into Alice in Wonderland, 'and I want to congratulate you – and encourage you. I wonder if you'd
let me have a look round? By the way, this is my
grand-niece, Alison Foster, and I don't think I told
you, my name is Major Foster.

'Oh thank you – how do you do – I mean, of course –
yes, if you like,' I mumbled, all in one breath, and
then pulled myself together and wondered where on
earth Bar and Pat had got to – they were probably
hiding on purpose – and said, 'Some of the horses are
out. The Shetland is giving a child a ride in the paddock, and there are two horses grazing in there. But
you can have a look at the stables with pleasure.'

So I took him into the stalls, and thank goodness
they were clean, and he seemed most impressed, and
when we got to the box stall at the end, there was
Pedro.

'Why, what's this?' said Major Foster, and I tried
to explain a bit, and before I knew where I was it was
all coming out, about the forty pounds Mummy had
given me to buy myself a jumper, and about how Bar
and I had gone to the sale at Farbury and bought
Begorra, and about how we had found Pedro with
the firewood cart, and all the rest.

Major Foster couldn't have been more interested or
nicer. He had a look at Pedro, and said, 'I think
you've got something here much better than you
think, but time will show' – which I thought was a

lovely, grown-uppish thing to say, as from one horsy person to another, and then he took out his notebook and scribbled something on a page and tore it out and gave it to me, saying, 'Get that made up at the chemist. It'll cure those harness galls before you can say knife.'

We came out into the yard, and Major Foster said, 'About Alison here. Her mother wants her to learn to ride, and so do I for that matter. What I wondered was, do you give lessons?'

'Well, this isn't a riding school,' I said, 'but I think we could teach Alison to ride. Both my partner and I are very experienced and have won a lot of firsts at shows.'

'Could she have a lesson now?' he said. 'And how much do you charge?'

'Oh, I don't know,' I said. 'I should think about twenty-five pence, if that isn't too much. If you like to leave her she can go up on Dot when that other child comes off, and when she's learned to sit properly and gets the feel of the saddle I'll teach her on Ballerina, who is the only properly schooled pony. Or would you like to wait?'

Major Foster said he would like to wait, so we went along to the paddock, and the first thing he said was, 'I say! What a fine-looking mare. And just my weight. Is that the one you bought yesterday? And have you got any tack for her?'

'Well, actually no,' I said, 'but there's a lot of tack

up at Uncle Toots' – I mean, he isn't my uncle but
that doesn't matter – and when Pat has time he's going
to fetch some down here for Begorra and perhaps for
Pedro too. As a matter of fact, we've only just got
Begorra here about a quarter of an hour ago and we
haven't tried her at all. She may be awful. Bar was
going to try her with Bungie's saddle this afternoon.'

'Then I shall certainly come back this afternoon,'
said Major Foster, 'and I don't think she's going to be

awful at all, and I intend to be your first customer for
Begorra, and I shall want her for an hour a day – if
not more.'

I opened my mouth, and shut it again, because I
really wanted to say that I couldn't let anybody
arrange to monopolize Begorra like that without
consulting my partners, but he must have read my
thoughts because he said, 'You see, I'm making a
nuisance of myself, but of course I shall pay you
double fees in compensation. And now I see that the
fat child has finished with Dot, so shall we see what
you can do with Alison?'

But just at that moment Bungie who was feeling
inquisitive ambled up to us and began to snuffle round
the pocket of Alison's jodhpurs as though in search of
apples or sugar. Alison was terrifically pleased and
threw her arms round Bungie's foreleg and held on,
yelling, 'I want this horse! I want to ride this horse!'

'Oh gosh, no, you can't learn on that horse,' I said,
'he's too big and he sags in the middle,' and Major
Foster said, 'There's a nice pony here for you, Alison,
just the thing to learn on, give you a good seat.'

But Alison who was apparently a very spoiled kid,
held on to Bungie all the tighter, and yelled, 'I want
this horse. I won't ride a pony! I'll ride this horse.'

I looked helplessly at Major Foster who shrugged
shoulders and said, 'She'll have to have her own way.
Make the best of it.'

So in the end I saddled Bungie and put Alison up,

and Major Foster leaned on the gate while I taught the kid to sit straight and keep her hands down, though I couldn't do much about her legs and feet, Bungie being the wrong shape for her. She seemed to have naturally light hands and soon learned to hold the reins correctly, and I walked her round the paddock and she squealed with joy, and after half an hour Major Foster said, 'Good! You'll make a rider of her yet. I'll bring her tomorrow at the same time, and you'd better see that that horse is out of the way and give her something she can get her knees into. And remember I shall want Begorra!'

He then solemnly handed me the twenty-five pence for Alison's lesson, and they went away both turning back to wave at the gate.

The minute they were gone, as I expected, Bar and Pat arrived from nowhere.

'What did he want?' they both asked excitedly.

'I've a jolly good mind not to tell you, walking out on me like that,' I said, but of course I couldn't resist, and soon I had told them the whole story.

'Oh, I do hope Begorra's all right,' said Bar. 'Pat, the minute after lunch, put Bungie's tack on to her and we'll all try her. I simply can't wait. Mike, if you've done with Dot, go and see if you can hurry Agatha up a bit with our lunch.'

So after lunch, Bar went up on Begorra and there wasn't the slightest doubt about her. She had a nice, smooth action and quite a bit of spirit too, and she seemed happy and at ease.

'You all right up there?' yelled Pat. 'Any snow on the top?'

'Oh, she does feel high!' said Bar. 'But it's lovely. And she's narrow too and very comfortable. Look out, I'm going to do trot, canter, and gallop.'

So Bar put Begorra through her paces without any trouble, and then I had a try, and then Pat – though Pat wasn't so successful as Begorra didn't seem to like his jockey style of riding.

'We'd better cut out the gallop,' I said. 'She's panting like old boots, but she's full of spirit and she'll make a beautiful, easy hack if she isn't over-ridden. I think Major Foster will take good care of her; he understands horses.'

So Pat went off to Uncle Toots' on Ballerina to fetch the other tack, and Bar and Mike and I looked after the stable.

13 - Cecilia's birthday

I HAD before me next day the exciting prospect of showing Pedro the paddock for the first time, but luckily I remembered that it was also Cecilia's birthday. Actually I could hardly have forgotten, because when I got back Auntie P. was in the kitchen icing a birthday cake, and on the hall table was a parcel labelled 'To Cecilia, not to be opened till tomorrow.'

So in the silent watches of the night I worked furiously to finish the Fair Isle gloves which still wanted two fingers and a thumb on the left hand, but I got them finished and they really did look snappy, with a natural ground and a very complicated pattern in black, green, red and white. Cecilia was so thrilled with them that I nearly fell down flat with the shock. She and my aunt seemed to be completely overcome by the fact that I could do Fair Isle knitting as well as things with horses, and they kept saying things like, 'When you can do such beautiful Fair Isle knitting, how can you *bear* to mess your hands up in stables?' – which I couldn't see the point of. I mean, it's all right to do Fair Isle knitting in the long winter evenings, but to my way of thinking the summer is given us for much higher things.

However Cecilia said that apart from the gold charm bracelet which her father and mother had given her, she liked my present better than anything else she had had, which didn't seem to me to be saying much as the rest of her presents were such squalid things as pink satin coat-hangers, a handkerchief case, and a book called 'Friends of the Lower Fifth'.

However both Cecilia and my aunt were in a frightfully good temper, and so was I as I had had a long letter from Mummy in answer to one of mine about the stable.

Cecilia said I must be sure to promise to be back for her birthday party at four o'clock, and I said I would. I would have promised anything as I was in such a hurry to get to Pedro and see how he was.

When I got to the vicarage Bar was dashing about with a bucket, and she shouted to me, 'What do you think of that?' waving in the direction of Pedro's box. He was actually standing there with his head over the half door, taking an interest in what was going on. When he saw me he pricked up his ears and a sort of welcoming look dawned on his plain features.

'We've fed him,' said Bar. 'We couldn't resist.'

'That's okay,' I said. 'I can't wait to get him out to grass.'

So I opened the door and got Pedro's halter rope and led him out, with Bar, Pat, and Mike clustering round and we opened the gate of the paddock and sort of urged him in.

He stood just inside with a look on his face like you might have if you suddenly found yourself transported to scenes of tropical splendour. He had a long, slow look round, and then down at his feet as much as to say, 'Gosh, grass!' Then a look of terrific bliss shivered all over him and he put his head down and got a mouthful and munched.

It was a thrilling moment for us and gave me for one a bucked-up feeling as I'd always wanted to do this for a horse that wasn't having a good time in life and now I'd done it.

'He'll be all right,' said Pat. 'Go on, Pedro, get farther in, it's all yours.'

This last remark was necessary as Pedro was more than a bit stunned and remained standing just inside the paddock gate, eating the part round his feet.

So we all gave him a friendly shove and he went farther in, but I bet if he could have rubbed his eyes he would have done so.

'Well that's that,' said Bar. 'We've got work to do.'

So we started getting the other horses ready for the

clients, and then as we weren't very busy that morning
Bar and I had a ride ourselves, she on Ballerina and I
on Begorra – who was lovely to ride, though so high
that I had to have shoving behind to mount her. It
was a crisp, fresh sort of morning and we went to the
common and let the horses enjoy themselves, and I
could almost believe that I was on Black Boy at

home and that Bar was my friend Ann. It occurred
to me that I was leading what is known as a double
life, and though I liked this half of it very much I

should be wild with joy to get back to my real one. I had a letter from Ann the day before which made me feel quite homesick.

She wrote: 'I am awfully glad you have got horsy friends and I hope you have got riding too by now. I have been to Mrs. Darcy's twice to see Black Boy and he looks awfully happy, I hope this won't make you feel depressed because I expect he is really longing for you and hiding a broken heart with a smiling face, as they say. No, Susan Pyke didn't win anything at all at the show – can you believe that! – I think her star is on the wane (that's out of history and means Julius Caesar really), and I got second in the showing class under fourteen and commended in the jumping, but it wasn't half such fun without you, and won't it be super when you come back? Yours ever, Ann.'

In the afternoon Major Foster arrived, true to his word, for his ride with Begorra and brought Alison for her lesson. Off he went, while Alison hung back and said, 'I want my big horse' – meaning Bungie.

'She'll have to have him,' I said to Bar.

'Rot,' said Bar. And she fixed Alison with an eagle eye and said, 'Look here, kid, you're going on the Shetland and you're jolly well going to like it.'

I had never heard Bar sound so sergeant-majorish and Alison looked flattened out. I don't think anybody before in her life had ever told that spoiled kid what she had to do. She stood meekly by while Bar led out

Dot and helped her to mount, and then Mike came to take her into the paddock for her lesson. There she sat with her mouth wide open, staring back at Bar but doing just as she was told by Mike, a pleasant sight to see.

'She's settled,' said Bar dusting off her hands. 'We'll have no more nonsense from her. I think I'd make a jolly good riding mistress, don't you?' Then she suddenly stood as though thunder-struck and said, 'Will you look at that?'

It was Pedro. He had been quietly grazing on the far side of the paddock, now he lifted his head and looked in an interested way at Dot, then suddenly set off at a beautiful canter towards her, brushing the grass so lightly that he nearly seemed to fly.

'Look at that action!' cried Bar. 'He's going to be a lovely pony.'

I felt so happy as I looked at Pedro that I went all choky in the throat. He stopped a few yards away from Dot and began to crop grass again, but he had shown us what he could do and we were quite certain that he had once belonged to people who had cared for him and schooled him properly, and how he came into the horrible hands of J. Biggs we should never know, unless he had been stolen or sold by soulless persons who didn't trouble to inquire about the kind of home he was going to. I thought it was a pity that Pedro couldn't write his own story which would probably make a much better book than any I write.

Then Major Foster came back, simply beaming all over and crooning Begorra's praises, and when he saw Alison on Dot he said, 'How on earth did you manage that?'

'Oh, just knack,' said Bar. 'It's all part of running a stable.'

At which Major Foster ha-ha-ed and said, 'Same time tomorrow,' and paid for Alison's lesson and his own ride, and went off looking like a sworn friend of Walters and Crewe Ltd.

Our clients finished fairly early that day and Mike came running out of the house with his camera and said, 'I've got a whizzo idea. Let's put the horses in their boxes with their six heads over the half-doors and we'll all line up in front and Agatha can take a photo of us. Then we can send it to *Country Life* or *Horse and Hound* and they'll probably put it on the front page instead of Lady Somebody.'

We agreed to this, but believe me, it took blue ages to organize, and the human beings were worse than the horses, as we had to wash and brush our hair and straighten our ties and get some whitewash off Bar's shoulder, to say nothing of getting round Agatha to come out and take the photograph. Then when we were finally arranged Pat would keep dashing out of line to take another imaginary sweat mark off Mipsy's neck.

'I can't get you all in,' said Agatha.

'Well, back a bit,' said Pat.

'I am backing,' said Agatha. 'If I back any more I'll be in the swill bucket.'

Eventually she got jammed against the house wall and couldn't back another inch.

'Which thing do I press down?' she said next.

'I'll come and show you,' said Mike, so he did.

When he got back into line Agatha said, 'Do I bring it up again when I've pressed it down?'

'It comes back automatically, you dope,' said Pat.

'Don't you speak to me like that,' said Agatha, 'or I'll have nothing to do with your camera.'

'Shut up, Pat,' said Bar. 'We apologize, Agatha. Go on, be quick.'

'Oh,' said Mike, 'we ought to have Slap and the cats in.' And he rushed off to find these animals. Slap their fox terrier about whom I have previously said nothing was a dog of awful character about whom volumes could be written by anybody who writes dog books, and there was a very big spoiled cat belonging to Agatha, called Edward, and a little grey cat which had rashly adopted the Walters'.

At last Mike appeared dragging all these animals along, and he arranged them with great care in front of our feet, but needless to say they weren't having any and after we had wasted about ten minutes on them they all mooched away.

So Agatha took the picture, and then another to make sure. Then Pat said, 'I don't believe you turned the film,' and she hadn't, so those two were wasted and she had to take another, which was the last on the film.

To complete this story, when we got the print from the chemist the following week it was rather disappointing. To begin with, Agatha hadn't got it all in and Pedro and Ballerina who occupied the stalls at each end were off altogether. Bungie and Begorra were very good, but Dot had put her head down at the crucial moment and only her ears showed, and Mipsy had shoved his nose forward and looked more like an elephant than a horse. As for us, Pat and I were quite good, but Mike had moved, and what struck you most about Bar was the patch of whitewash on her shoulder which she hadn't got out as successfully as she thought she had. There was a sort of wavy thing across one corner which we couldn't place at all until at last Agatha realized that it was Edward's tail just disappearing as he made his dash for liberty.

So *Country Life* and *Horse and Hound* were done out of the marvellous picture they were going to get for their front page, and Lady Somebody was in as usual.

However to get back to the moment when the photograph had actually been taken, I looked at my watch and said, 'Help, it's a quarter past four!' And I remembered I had promised to be at Cecilia's birthday party which began at four. So I dashed off like mad and arrived at the house at a quarter to five. I could see the party inside sitting round the tea table. I flew upstairs, sloshed a bit of water on my hands, dragged a comb through my hair, tore off my shirt and pulled on my blue frock. All this only took about eighteen seconds and then I burst into the dining-room feeling as if flames were coming out of my ears and said, 'I'm frightfully sorry I'm late.'

'You certainly are late,' said my aunt with a sort of iciness under the sweetness. 'There's your place,' and I slunk into a chair between two girls I didn't know who didn't offer to pass me anything but just stared, so I helped myself to the last sandwich on the plate, and then Cecilia cut her cake which had pink candles on it and everybody beamed at her and they sang 'Happy Birthday to You' which I thought was too soppy for words.

Then tea was over and we all got up and went to the drawing-room to play guessing jumbled fruits, and just as I was wondering why if they had to jumble something they didn't jumble something decent like kinds of horses, there was a roar of laughter and to my horror I realized that everybody was laughing at me!

I couldn't think what was wrong, and then I happened to glance down and the awful truth was revealed. I had forgotten to take off my jodhpurs when

I put on my blue frock, and there they were below the blue hem looking most peculiar. I could have gone through the floor, especially when Cecilia said, 'Oh, it's just like Jill, she's quite crazy,' and all the horrible girls from her horrible school tittered and giggled. All except one who to everybody's surprise said, 'Never mind, Jill – you are called Jill, aren't you? – I know just how you feel because the same thing once happened to me, only much worse because it was at a garden party my mother was giving, all bristling with important people. So just stop laughing, everybody.'

And this girl came over to me and said – while all the others listened with pricked up ears – 'Aren't you the girl who's running a very successful hacking stable over at Matley? I'm awfully interested, do tell me about it. Never mind your jodhpurs, you can take them off after.'

It turned out that her name was Mary Dangerfield and she was the head of the school and terribly popular, what was more Cecilia had a crush on her and everything that Mary did was just right.

So while I was telling Mary about the stable and she was listening in a very interested way, you should have seen Cecilia's face! And after a bit she came up and said, 'Jill knows an awful lot about horses. You don't ride, do you, Mary?'

'Of course I do,' said Mary, 'but I don't suppose I'm a patch on Jill. I've never had the nerve to go in for show jumping!' And then she added, 'Do let me come round to Matley and see your stable some time,' and I said, 'Yes, do come, whenever you like.'

From that day Cecilia and Auntie P. were quite different to me and treated me as the sort of person Mary Dangerfield thought worth knowing. Which is very silly really, but it just shows you!

And it was much nicer for me and I was jolly glad I'd forgotten to change my jodhpurs.

14 - A great day at the stable

I CAN'T go into details about all the things we did in the next two or three weeks. That is the worst of writing a book, if you put every single thing in it would be as big as an encyclopedia, and yet you hate to leave anything out, and quite a lot of funny as well as rather paralysing things happened at the stable that I haven't time to describe.

One thing I must admit is that while we went on doing all the work that had to be done each day we were all secretly deciding that we didn't want to run a stable for the rest of our lives. It is funny how you get cured of things, isn't it? Bar said that she thought she would have a stab at being a commercial artist and doing railway posters which had a fascination for her, and Mike said he still wanted to be a vet because they had somebody to muck out and groom for them, and he thought it would be fun to do things to dogs for a change.

Pat said, 'You'd probably have to set old ladies' parrots' broken legs all the time,' and Mike said he'd quite like even that.

We spent a lot of time improving the horses, except for Bungie who was past improving. Mike did wonders with Mipsy and Dot, schooling them both for part of each day, while Begorra proved to be a very nice jumper. She was popular with our older clients, as well as with Major Foster who had her out most afternoons.

I spent all the time I could spare with Pedro, because it was such fun to see him gradually remembering things he had been taught in his happier days. He was a nice pony to ride and very appreciative of anything you did for him. We discovered that he understood bending and musical chairs, though he was out of practice of course, and we wondered more than ever about the secret of his past, alas, never to be disclosed. The look of misery had quite gone from his eyes and he was filling out and his coat improving, and he had all the makings of a good pony.

So the weeks sped by, and one day when we were cleaning up at the end of the afternoon Bar said, 'I do wish something would happen to pep things up a bit.'

'Listen to this,' said Pat who was reading the local paper, sitting on an upturned bucket, 'It says, "According to the annual custom, the Earl of Sattingham's stables were open to the public last Saturday in aid of local hospitals. The Police Band was in attendance and rendered selections. Patrons included Lord and Lady — Something, etc. etc. etc." There you are!

That's the thing we ought to do, have the stable open for inspection and invite all our clients.'

We looked round at each other to see how the idea was sinking in, and Bar said, 'It would be rather fun. They could bring their parents and things, to make a few more.'

'We'd have to have tea,' said Pat, 'or at least buns and lemonade. I wonder if Agatha would co-operate?'

'What shall it be in aid of?' I asked.

'Oh, horses in general.'

'You can't just say horses in general.'

'Well, say our horses in particular.'

'I'll tell you what,' said Bar, 'that thing Mummy went to at the Institute said "to promote friendship throughout the world". Couldn't we just say, "to promote the welfare of horses throughout the world" and then we could send the money to the Blue Cross?'

'Oh, *bong!*' I said. 'We ought to have some invitation cards. We could buy ordinary postcards and print them ourselves.'

'We could save a bit of money on that,' said Pat practically, 'by using Daddy's sermon paper which is just the right size for invitations and quite thick. I know where there's a whole drawer of it.'

'Will he mind?' I said.

'Oh, I'll stand the racket, if any,' said Pat.

So while Agatha was busy upstairs we all oozed

into the absent vicar's study and found a large wad of
the sermon papers.

Then we drafted out an invitation which read:

WALTERS AND CREWE LTD
invite you to inspect their model stables
next Wednesday afternoon at 3
Afternoon Tea
Price 5p or anything you like to give
Proceeds in aid of promoting the welfare of horses
throughout the world

I thought the last sentence might have been better
expressed as it wasn't very neat, but we couldn't think
of anything better so we let it stand. We all thought
that Bar was a bit rash putting in Afternoon Tea
without consulting Agatha, but Pat said if the worst
came to the worst we could make some lemonade
ourselves with lemonade crystals and water, and buy
a few buns.

However to our surprise when we approached
Agatha she seemed to cotton on to the idea like anything. I suppose she thought it would brighten her
dull existence to see the yard glittering with gay
social life, and she said she would make tea and
provide the cups and saucers only we would have to
buy the food ourselves as the housekeeping didn't
stretch to feeding swarms of people.

So then we all sat down round the vicar's desk and

started copying out the invitations. We decided to do three dozen and include a few people we knew who weren't exaclty clients, like Mary Dangerfield and Uncle Toots' locum.

'We'll have to watch Mike,' said Bar, 'or he'll spell words wrong.'

'I will not!' shouted Mike indignantly.

I kept an eye on him without him noticing me, and he was most careful, looking at the copy card for every single word, but at the end when we had finished it was four of Bar's cards that we had to scrap as she had forgotten the Afternoon Tea line and had spelt 'throughout', throgut.

Next day we distributed the invitations to our clients and they were frightfully thrilled and said they would all come and bring their parents. We then realized what a frightful lot of work we had let ourselves in for, getting the stables ready for inspection. We scrubbed and scoured and polished, and swilled the yard.

We asked Agatha if we could have the tea in the drawing-room, but she took a dim view of this, and said that if it was a wet day on Saturday she'd have a week's work taking up the footmarks to say nothing of millions of crumbs trodden into the carpet. Then to soften the blow she said she would find time to make some shortbread biscuits.

'Tell you what,' said Pat, 'we'll put the tea in the

harness room. We can take all the stuff out and put the kitchen table in the middle with all the plates of food laid out on it, and everybody can rally round and help themselves like they did at that potty wedding of Cousin Sheila's that Mother made us go to.'

'Oh yes, a buffet,' I said.

So we made the harness room look as nice as we could, and Agatha said we needn't take the kitchen table, we could have the gate-leg one out of the morning room, so we put it up and laid a clean cloth on it, and Bar and I picked some dahlias and put them in a jug to go in the middle. It looked very nice. However, that same evening, which was the night before the party, a most ghastly thing happened. Over the harness room was the loft where we kept the straw and Mike had gone up to get some, forgetting that the flooring was a bit dicky, and his foot went right through and heaps of plaster and spiders and straw and chaff fell down on the beautiful table underneath.

You never saw such a mess. We groaned and groaned, and then we had to set to work and clean it all up again – which took hours – and Mike had to get round Agatha for another clean cloth, and I didn't get home till half past nine and Auntie P. was far from pleased, and we nearly wished the inspection at blazes.

But the great day dawned at last and it was fine. We

had told our clients there would be no riding that morning, and we set to work and groomed the horses till they fairly glittered and washed their tails with 'Gleemit', of which we had bought ourselves a bottle, seeing how successful it was, and we tethered them all in the paddock in the shade of the trees so that nothing awful could happen to them.

Then Bar and I rushed down to the confectioner's shop in Matley village to buy the food. We bought two dozen teacakes and six dozen mixed buns, which we thought should be enough, but when we got home with them and Agatha saw the tea cakes she said, 'What am I supposed to spread on these? Not your father's butter, I hope?'

So we decided to spread jam on them and Mike said he would do it, though he rather overdid it and the jam oozed out and a lot of wasps gathered round, but it might have been worse.

At last everything was ready and it did look good.

I don't know whether you have ever arranged an affair of this kind, but I remember Mummy saying that one of two things always happens, either too few people turn up or too many.

Ours was one of the 'too many' occasions.

I suppose our clients' parents were all interested and wanted to see for themselves what the stable was like, and then people like Mary Dangerfield came because they thought it would be fun, and a lot of public-minded people that we hadn't actually invited came along because they wanted to do something for the welfare of horses throughout the world.

It was all right when they started arriving in twos – because for a minute during our scrappy lunch we had had an awful feeling that perhaps nobody would come at all – but when they started coming in sixes our blood ran cold, as the saying goes.

We thought perhaps they would walk round the stables, cast an eye over the horses in the paddock, eat a bun and go, but they didn't. They stayed, and more and more came.

'What on earth are we going to do with them?' said Bar.

'Oh, let them rip,' I said. 'They're enjoying themselves, strange as it seems.'

The paddock now looked like a showground.

'Shall we start giving rides?' said Pat, and this proved to be an excellent idea. Everybody who was dressed for it – and heaps of people were in shorts or jodhpurs – wanted rides, and presently there was a continuous line of horses going round the paddock.

'This is a great affair!' cried Major Foster, bustling up with Alison and Alison's fond mother. 'Why, the whole neighbourhood is here. You kids ought to congratulate yourselves.'

'Yes, but we don't know what's going to happen when they get to the tea and bun stage,' said Bar.

'We only allowed for about forty and there are at least eighty.'

'Oh, don't worry about that,' said the Major, and he whispered something to Alison's mother who afterwards melted away, and about ten minutes later returned with several bags of cakes.

'Oh thank you!' cried Bar, rushing off to the harness room to add this wealth to the buffet at which by now some people were hungrily looking.

'You'll never get everybody round that table,' said the Major. 'Why not bring it out into the yard? It will look more festive and everybody will be able to get at it.'

We thought this was a good idea, so the Major and Pat and a few others carried out the table into the middle of the yard, and just then out came Agatha with two enormous pots of tea, the pots being the ones they used at the church for Sunday school teas and harvest suppers and so on.

Mary Dangerfield came up to me and said, 'I do think this is fun. I've had a ride on Ballerina and the Walters boy told me all about you buying Pedro. Isn't Cecilia here?'

'She would have come,' I said, 'but there's a dancing display at her dancing class.'

'What weird tastes some people have!' said Mary in a very friendly woman-to-woman way, and I thought that when I got home at night and told

Cecilia that Mary had been there she would be green with fury that she had stayed away for a silly dancing display.

The next minute I heard Mike ringing a bell and everybody stopped talking, and then Major Foster stood up on the old mounting block and said, 'We can hardly let this occasion go by without thanking our hosts and hostesses for this very delightful entertainment they have so kindly arranged for us. Those of us who love horses couldn't ask for any improvements in these model stables and the way the horses here are looked after, and I for one would like to move

a vote of thanks to Walters and Crewe Ltd. who have the welfare of horses throughout the world so much at heart.'

Everybody clapped like mad, and then Major Foster himself picked up an empty plate – they were all empty by now! – and began taking the collection. The silver simply rained in and it was obvious that everybody was giving more than a penny. (Actually the collection came to nine pounds sixty-five and when we had paid ourselves back for the buns and things we sent eight pounds seventy-five to the Blue Cross Fund for Horses and got an awfully nice letter back which we stuck up with adhesive tape on the inside of the harness room door.)

Then all of a sudden Bar said, 'Oh help, here are some more people!'

Eleven late comers were just coming in at the gate.

'There isn't a thing left to eat,' I said.

'Have you any money?' said Bar.

'Only about eightpence,' I said.

'Well, look,' said Bar, 'we can't possibly worry Major Foster with this. You nip down to the shop and get about eighteen mixed cakes as quick as you can whizz, and tell them we'll pay them on Saturday. They ought to know us by now. Meanwhile I'll try and get round Agatha to make just one more pot of tea. We can't possibly spoil this splendiferous do by turning the hungry from our door.'

With that she rushed off to welcome the newcomers who proved to be Diana and Brenda Prince with their father and mother and kid sister, and a boy called Bill Manners with what looked like the whole of his family.

15 - I am knocked for six

I SEIZED the nearest bike – which happened to be Pat's – and did the half-mile to the confectioner's in under two minutes, bought the cakes, and came back pedalling hard up the hill, holding the bag of cakes in one hand and coping with the peculiar steering habits of Pat's bike with the other.

As I got to the gate of the stable yard I noticed a tall, youngish clergyman with black curly hair standing looking in rather a stunned way at the notice board which said Walters and Crewe, Hacks for Hire.

I slid off the bike and said, 'Can I do anything for you?'

'Yes,' he said, 'what's the meaning of this?'

'It's a hacking stable,' I said kindly. 'Walters and Crewe. I'm one of the partners, Crewe.'

'Oh are you?' he said in a peculiar tone. 'And what are all these people doing?' – waving his hand to the scene of gay activity in the yard where certainly a lot of people seemed to be milling about, though some had gone home by now.

'It's an open day,' I explained. 'There's a tea, and

the stables are on view. You can come in if you like.'

'Oh, can I!' he said. I thought he had a very strange manner and seemed to talk in questions.

Just then Pat hove into view leading Pedro with Alison Foster up and Alison's fond mother fluttering around her.

'Patrick!' the clergyman fairly roared. 'Come here this minute!'

Pat looked round.

'Oh, hullo, Daddy,' he said in a rather wilted voice.

Well, actually you could have knocked me for six. So this was the Walters' father! Actually I had always pictured the absent vicar with a long white beard and tottering on two sticks.

Mr. Walters strode into the yard and said, 'Where are Barbara and Michael?'

They detached themselves from the crowd, and quite a lot of people said, 'Hullo, Mr. Walters', while his three progeny (as children are sometimes called) stood around and waited and I hovered near.

'Now what have you been up to?' said Mr. Walters, looking round at all the people and the remains of the tea and horses all over the place, and not unnaturally overcome, having left everything so dead and dirty and peaceful when he went away.

'Oh please, Daddy, let everybody get away,' said Bar, 'and then we'll explain.'

At last everybody had gone and we were left with

just the six horses, and Agatha helping to clear up the cups and things.

'Really!' said the vicar. 'I don't know what the bishop would say.'

'Well, it just depends whether he's in favour of free enterprise,' said Bar, which I thought was rather good. 'We're running a stable and it's very successful and self-supporting and these people who've been here to tea are our clients and their parents and friends, and I do hope you don't mind, Daddy –'

'– because the whole idea,' went on Pat, 'was to make Ballerina earn her keep so you wouldn't sell her when you came back –'

'– and she has done, and I hope you won't,' finished Mike.

'This beats me,' said the vicar. 'Whose idea was it?'

'I'm afraid it was mine,' I said, chipping in for the first time.

'Break it gently,' said the vicar. 'Who are you? How dare you put ideas into my children's innocent minds?'

I began to giggle, and Bar said, 'Innocent minds my foot!'

'I'm Jill Crewe,' I said quite seriously, 'and I'm staying here with my aunt, and I know what it feels like to think you are going to lose your pony because you can't afford to keep him – or her – because I've had it myself, so naturally I had to think of a plan to keep Ballerina from being sold, and this was it.'

'Naturally!' said the vicar. 'Naturally!'

'It was a jolly good plan,' said Pat, 'and it worked.'

'But where on earth did you get all these horses?'

'Three of them are from Uncle Toots,' said Mike, 'and Jill bought the other two for the stable. Begorra's a hunter, isn't she smashing? And I must tell you about Pedro –' and off he went into an absolute jumble about J. Biggs and all the rest of it.

'And what has Agatha had to say about all this?' asked the vicar.

'Oh, Agatha isn't a bit to blame,' said Bar hastily. 'She was against it from the beginning but of course she couldn't actually stop us.'

'Come in the house,' said the vicar, and we all followed him to the study.

'I've had my breath taken away,' he said, looking round at us, 'but you don't seem to have done anything very frightful. Of course you'd better go and get that board down before your mother comes home tomorrow, and this whole thing will have to stop immediately. The bishop would have a fit.'

We all looked at each other.

'It seems a bit sudden,' said Mike.

'I don't know what the clients will think,' said Pat.

'Never mind that,' said the vicar. 'This is hereby the end of Walters and Crewe, not forgetting the Ltd. I'm glad *something* was limited. This is a vicarage, not a hacking stable or any other kind of stable. Do you know you are not supposed to run commercial enterprises on vicarage property?'

'Good afternoon,' said a sudden voice, and the face and form of Major Foster appeared at the window. 'I suppose you are the vicar?'

'To my sorrow,' said the harassed parent of Bar, Pat, and Mike.

'Well, I'm Major Foster, and I just wanted to tell you that in my opinion these young people have put up a first-class show. I heard what you were saying, and I daresay the whole thing has been a little irregular and will have to come to an end, but I have nothing but praise for the way these four have worked, kept everything clean and on a business footing, and looked after their six horses.'

'Oh, thank you, Major Foster!' cried Pat. 'Did you hear that, Daddy?'

'Well, well!' said the vicar. 'You children seem to have made a good impression on *somebody*.'

'A very good impression,' said Major Foster, suddenly putting one leg over the windowsill and climbing into the room. He then introduced himself properly to Mr. Walters and went on, 'If this business is to be wound up here and now, please let me be in at the winding.'

'Oh, thank you, Major Foster,' said Bar, Mike, and I simultaneously.

'You people look a bit blue,' said Major Foster. 'What's the trouble?'

'We've got an awful lot of horses on our hands,' I said, because I felt particularly blue, realizing that Begorra and Pedro were my slightly unwanted property and wondering what on earth I was going to do with them.

'I suppose Bungie and Mipsy and Dot can go back to Uncle Toots',' said Pat, 'but they will find their lives dull after having such a good time with the clients.'

'Oh Bar,' I said, 'do you think your father will let Begorra and Pedro stay here for just a little while? I don't know what on earth to do with them. I don't really want them for myself, but I can't bear to think of sending them to some sordid auction room where they might even be bought by that foul Mr. Biggs or somebody just as soulless. I mean, for the poor things just to have got away from such beastly surroundings into all this, and then to go back again —'

By now I was nearly choking, and I must have sounded frightfully eloquent because Bar snatched at her hanky and even Pat and Mike gave snorts like boys do when they would cry if they weren't boys.

'Jill!' cried the Major. 'I mean, Miss Crewe. Just put all ideas like that out of your head. I've got it all arranged. Nobody is going to ride Begorra but me. She suits me down to the ground, and if you'll sell her to me I'll be proud to have her. Will you?'

'Oh Major Foster!' I nearly yelled. 'How absolutely terrific of you!'

'And what's more,' he went on, 'I'm going to buy Pedro too, for Alison's birthday present. The kid will love him and he's a grand little pony.'

By this time I was knocked for six, Bar and Pat and Mike were beaming with excitement, and even the vicar said, 'I'm getting interested in this in spite of myself'.

'Now then,' said Major Foster, 'I'm quite sure there isn't going to be any meal in this house tonight suitable for a family reunion and the winding up of a successful business, so I suggest you all come to the *George* as my guests for dinner.'

This suggestion seemed to us the last word in luxurious goings on, so Bar, Pat, and Mike flew upstairs to wash and change while I went to ring my aunt and see what sort of a view she took of it. It turned out that my aunt had heard of Major Foster and he was quite an Important Person – which meant a lot more to her than it did to me because I choose my friends for their niceness and mostly they are quite Unimportant Persons – so she not only said I might go but suggested I should go straight home and change and my uncle would actually run me over to the *George* in the car! I felt like a film star by now. So we got to the *George* and the dining-room was marvellous,

with branching candlesticks coming out of the walls and electric candles that looked just like real ones, and pictures of country scenes hung up, and there were round tables with white cloths and vases of Dorothy Perkins, and real waiters in white coats with table napkins over their arms.

We had a sumptuous dinner and all chose different things to make it more exciting – we thought at first this might be considered a bit rude, but Major Foster said, 'Go ahead' – and finished up with coffee and milk-shakes and a silver dish full of sugared fruits and things. It was terrific.

Then Bar – who was getting a bit keen on art said, 'Do you think we could go and look at the pictures on the walls?'

So all the Walters went to look at the pictures, but Major Foster said to me, 'Just a minute, I want a word with you, Miss Crewe'.

I stayed behind, and he said, 'Now shall you and I get down to the sordid question of cash?'

'Well, it is rather important,' I said. 'You see, the money I spent on buying Begorra who I did want and Pedro who I didn't want was what Mummy gave me to buy a show jumper. So all that money's gone now, and Mummy might take a dim view.'

'Very well,' he said. 'Now I don't know what you gave for Begorra, but I know what she's worth to me. I'll give you forty pounds for her.'

'Oh!' I said. 'But I –'

'That's settled,' he said firmly. 'Forty pounds for Begorra. I know what you gave for Pedro, five pounds. But Pedro now is a very different proposition from when you bought him. You've fed him, groomed him, given him some schooling, and made an attractive pony out of him. I'll give you twenty pounds for him That makes sixty pounds altogether. Satisfied?'

'Oh, Major Foster,' I said, 'it's too much.'

'Rubbish,' he said. 'I've got two good horses. It's a fair bargain.'

So it was settled. What an evening!

16 - There's a coincidence!

I WENT round to the stable next morning as usual, though I didn't know quite what was going to happen. After all, the horses had to be groomed and fed even if Fate was about to fling them far and wide. We turned them out to grass, and then Bar and I rang up all the clients. It must have cost a lot of money on the telephone account, and I hope the bishop helped out, as in a way it was for his benefit to save him from having a fit.

Then we wandered sort of aimlessly out into the yard where Mike was talking over the gate to Mipsy and saying, 'Oh poor Mipsy, you're going back to grass feeding and not being groomed any more, oh poor Mipsy'.

'Won't it seem empty when they've gone?' said Bar. 'I suppose we'll have to take them back before long. I never thought I could get really fond of Bungie and Mipsy and Dot, but I have, and we never got down to calling them Starlight and Cameron and Gay Girl, did we?'

'Do you think your Father would mind if we had one last ride?' I said sadly, and Bar said she was sure he wouldn't only he was in his study and hadn't to be disturbed, so we saddled up, and Pat rode Begorra, Bar rode Ballerina, I went on Pedro and Mike on Mipsy, and we had a marvellous canter on the common with the wind streaming through our hair and that wonderful feeling that only riding can give you.

When we got back there were Mr. Walters and Major Foster in the yard.

'Here they come!' cried the Major. 'Had a good ride, people? How did my two nags go?'

And as if they knew, Begorra and Pedro made straight for the Major who took lumps of sugar out of his pockets and gave it to them.

'I've got an idea,' he said, 'and that's why I came over. I thought it would wind everything up very nicely if you people came over to Woodbury Hall for tea on Saturday afternoon. My nephew and niece, Alison's parents, extend you a very hearty invitation and that includes Mr. and Mrs. Walters, and *your* aunt and uncle and cousin, Jill. And my niece is going to invite about twenty people she knows who have ponies and we'll get up a few open events like musical chairs and bending races, so the horses will have to come too. Two of you can ride Begorra and

Pedro and then hand them over to me. How does that strike you?'

'How absolutely gorgeous!' Bar and Pat and I yelled in chorus, and Mike said, 'Wow!' and fell flat on his back.

Then he got up again and said, 'Is there going to be jumping? Oh Major Foster, do let me help to make the jumps.'

'Don't you let him, Major Foster,' said Bar. 'Last time he made some jumps they looked so beastly edible that the ponies just stood still and munched.'

'I don't think we'll have any jumping on Saturday,' said Major Foster, 'because we haven't any jumps at Woodbury Hall, but you might be drafting out a schedule of the sort of events that anybody can go in for, regardless of age or type of pony.'

Then he took me on one side and handed me a bulgy envelope, saying, 'There's your money, in pound notes. Would you like to count it and see it's right?'

'Oh, I don't think I'll bother,' I said, and he laughed.

'Now put it carefully in your pocket,' he said, as though I were six, 'and when you get home give it to your aunt to take care of.'

What an idea!

When I got home and told Auntie P. and Cecilia about the invitation to Woodbury Hall on Saturday they were thrilled, but instead of helping me with ideas for some events in the pony show they could talk about nothing but what they would wear. As if anybody would look at them when there were ponies to watch!

Then Cecilia whispered something to Auntie P. and they both laughed mysteriously and began to whisper and giggle, and I thought they were slightly crazy but was too busy wondering how I was going to round up enough clean handkerchiefs for the handkerchief race to care about anything else.

Needless to say, everybody spent the whole of the next day, which was Friday, saying, 'Do you think it is going to be fine tomorrow?' because it looked a bit doubtful. However, the Met. Office must have relented and sent the deep depression packing off to Iceland or somewhere because Saturday turned out to be a lovely day with a slight mist in the morning and the sun just breaking through.

By one o'clock it was blazing, and I was ready dressed in my clean shirt and coat and jodhpurs, my boots polished by the gentle hand of Doris and rubbed up by my own, and I had done my hair in one plait and turned it up and tied it in a rather sophisticated way that Bar had showed me.

'You had better go on ahead, Jill,' said my aunt, 'and we will come along in the car later, probably about four o'clock.'

And she looked at Cecilia and they both giggled.

'That's awfully late,' I said to Cecilia, when she came to the door to see me off, 'you'll miss most of the events, but you'll be in time for tea,' and I thought that was probably all she cared about, which was misjudging her as you will see.

Everybody was buzzing around excitedly when I got to the stables.

'Oh, isn't it splendid,' shouted Bar. 'Daddy says we can keep Ballerina. So everything has been worth while, and it was all your idea in the first place and we're frightfully grateful, because if we had never met you we should still have been feebly moaning on a gate and Ballerina led away to the slaughter.'

'You'd have thought of something,' I said. 'How are we for money now the stable is closing down?'

'Just about evened out,' said Bar. 'There's two pounds owing to you which I'll give you today. And actually there's quite a lot of oats and bran and hay and stuff which belongs to us jointly.'

'Oh no,' I said. 'You keep that, Bar, please. It will give Ballerina a good start for the winter.'

'That's awfully decent of you,' said Bar. 'Now I actually haven't a care in the world. I do think the whole thing has been fun, don't you?'

'Terrific,' I agreed. 'Whatever should I have done if I hadn't met you people?'

Just then Mrs. Walters – who had arrived home the

day before – came out with a tray with glasses of iced lemonade which made a lovely start for the afternoon. She had on a grey skirt and blue blouse and looked much younger and prettier than vicars' wives usually look, owing to their cares. She and Mr. Walters were going to bike over to Woodbury Hall while we rode the horses.

'You do look nice,' she said to us all, 'and don't a lot of horses give an exciting look to a place? I never realized it before.'

I entirely agreed with this noble sentiment and liked Mrs. Walters ever after for saying it.

Then we all prepared to move off. I was riding Pedro again, as I had got used to him and wanted to be the one to try him in the pony events, and Bar had got Begorra, Pat was on Ballerina, and Mike on Mipsy. At the last minute we decided to take Bungie and Dot along too, to see the fun, so we led them.

Woodbury Hall was only about two miles away and was a lovely place with a large field at the side, just made for pony races, and a long line of what looked like stables at the side but proved to be nothing but sordid garages. Think of anybody being so soulless as to have stables and turn them into garages! But now that Alison was getting Pedro they would have to start turning them back into stables again, which was a step in the right direction.

Everything looked very gay, only I knew there was

going to be trouble when I saw Alison in a pair of new jodhpurs and a crash cap miles too big for her, and she made one wild dash for Pedro, taking it for granted she was going to ride. Of course I had to let her, and in the end I swallowed my disappointment and got up on Dot with my feet nearly touching the ground. I had wanted to try Pedro in the events for the first time, but after all he was going to be Alison's pony. Actually as it turned out, Alison couldn't keep her seat more than five minutes and Pedro wasn't any use without a skilled rider and they were last in everything, but they enjoyed themselves so much that I didn't mind any more, and Alison's mother said, 'Don't they look a lovely little pair? I'm sure they'll be winning everything together in a year or two.'

I had my doubts, but I do think the main thing in life is letting everybody be happy in their own way.

The lawn in front of the house was dotted with tea tables, and in the show field the poles were set up for the handkerchief race, and altogether it was a thrilling scene. About twenty people had brought ponies of all types and sizes, and among them was Mary Danger-field who came up and talked to me very chummily. She looked at Dot and laughed and said, 'You believe in keeping near the ground, don't you?' so I explained and we both laughed together.

In the end Bar, Pat, Mike and I got together and decided to pool horses and ride the better ones in turns. But when it came to the events Dot surprised us all. Not for nothing had she been ridden at many pony shows by the vet's daughter in her palmy days. She remembered her stuff, and Mike won the egg and spoon race on her while I was second in the bending.

Bar was first in the bending with Ballerina, and Pat was first in the flag race on Begorra, and I was first in the blind-fold rider race on Mipsy.

By half-past three everybody was breathless but happy, and though I had looked several times out of the corner of my eye I knew my aunt's party had not arrived which rather disappointed me.

'Now for the prizes,' said Major Foster. 'Everybody line up.'

It turned out that there were four prizes for each event, so everybody got at least one, even Alison who had won the Crazy Costume race, simply because everybody else had fallen off their ponies with laughing and she had stuck solemnly on and passed the post.

The prizes turned out to be very nice things. I got a silver propelling pencil that wrote red and green as well as black, and Bar got a wallet and diary all in one. Pat got a riding stick, and Mike a book called 'Two Boys and a Pony in Wild Wales'. Mary Dangerfield got a yellow tie and Alison got a pair of string gloves.

'And now,' said Major Foster, 'before we have

tea – for which everybody is dying – we'll have a Grand Parade. Twice round the field, please.'

So we took ten minutes to spruce up ourselves and the ponies, just like at a real show, and then we rode round in a ring carrying our prizes, and all the guests – for most people's parents were there – cheered and clapped. It was the best affair I had been to for ages.

Just as we completed the second round of the field I happened to glance towards the drive, and there drawing to a standstill was my uncle's car. It stopped, and out got my aunt, then Cecilia, and then not my uncle but somebody in a grey dress and a white hat.

My heart jumped right up in the air, turned over, and flopped back again. I couldn't believe it. I was dreaming or else I really had gone mad.

Then somehow I had tumbled off Mipsy and was whizzing across the grass pulling the astonished Mipsy with me and shouting, 'Mummy! oh, Mummy!'

Yes, it was my Mother, back from America. I still couldn't believe it.

'It's our surprise,' said Cecilia. 'We knew she was coming today, and we were going to the station to meet her at half-past three. We didn't tell you to make it more of a thrill.'

'I caught an earlier boat,' said Mummy, as we exchanged bear hugs.

'Well, if this isn't the most magnificent day of my life!' I said.

Ten minutes later we were sitting round a table on the lawn having tea, and I was doing most of the talking, telling Mummy all about the stable. Her story about America would keep till later.

Long before I got to the part about buying Begorra and Pedro she interrupted me and said, 'By the way, you haven't bought a show jumper yet, have you, Jill?'

'No, Mummy,' I said.

'That's good,' she said. 'Because on the boat coming over I met some people who told me of a pony they have for sale. He seems just the thing for you – a show jumper who has done well for their daughter but she is too old for the children's classes now. They

would like you to go over and give him a trial. Of course they want rather a lot of money for him – sixty pounds –'

She stopped and looked at me as though expecting me to say something.

'Gosh!' I said. 'Now *there's* a coincidence!'

THE SWISH OF THE CURTAIN

Pamela Brown

'The applause grew deafening, and gradually the people rose in their seats, still clapping. The theatre stood and cheered and stamped, while Lyn bowed and smiled for an eternity.'

This is the success which finally comes to the Blue Door Theatre Company, formed by a band of eager youngsters in their spare time. This book is the story of how and why they went about it, their set-backs and achievements.

This is a revised edition, specially done by Pamela Brown for Knight Books, of the book she originally wrote when she was fourteen years old. It has retained its popularity now for over twenty-five years.

These are other Knight Books

More books about horses and riding

Primrose Cumming
FOUR RODE HOME

Ruby Ferguson
JILL'S GYMKHANA
JILL HAS TWO PONIES
JILL ENJOYS HER PONIES
JILL AND THE PERFECT PONY
JILL'S RIDING CLUB
JILL'S PONY TREK

Mary Treadgold
THE HERON RIDE
RETURN TO THE HERON

Ask your local bookseller, or at your public library, for details of other Knight Books, or write to the Editor-in-Chief, Knight Books Arlen House, Salisbury Road, Leicester LE1 7QS